Adventure in Grand Canyon National Park

National Park Mystery Series

Book Three

Aaron Johnson

Illustrated by

The Author

Cover Artwork by Anne Zimanski

Illustrations by Aaron Johnson.

This is a work of fiction. Names, characters, organizations, historical events, and incidents are the products of the author's imagination. The roles played by historical figures and organizations in this narrative and their dialogue (while sometimes based on the known facts of their real lives) are also imagined. The snake in chapter one was not harmed in the writing of this narrative. In fact, Alexander Slithrington (that was his name) quite enjoyed his flight. He later took up base jumping and other extreme sports.

Paperback ISBN: 978-1-960053-01-5

Ebook ISBN: 978-1-960053-02-2

This book is dedicated to my Grandparents, James and Mary Johnson. Thank you for teaching me a love for flowers and a curiosity for all manner of growing things.

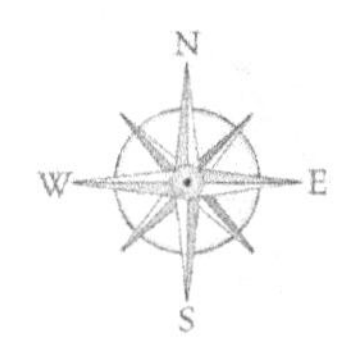

"Leave it as it is. You cannot improve on it. The ages have been at work on it, and man can only mar it."
- Theodore Roosevelt, Grand Canyon, 1903

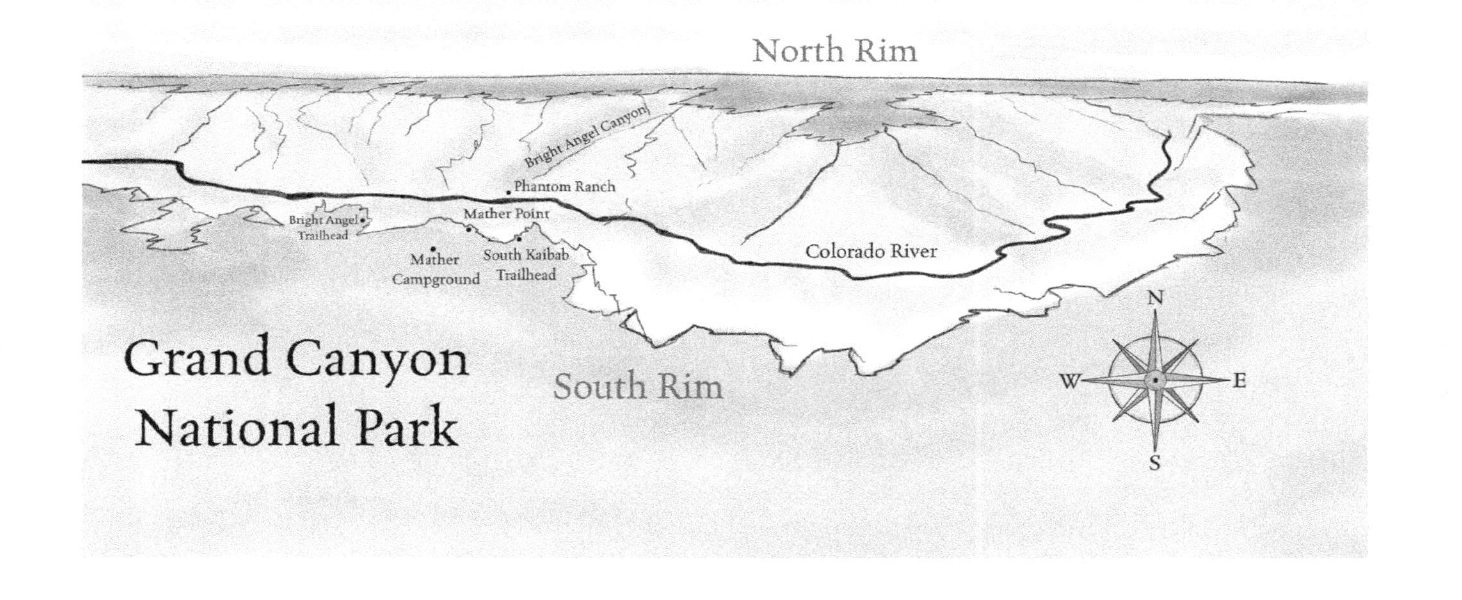
North Rim
Bright Angel Canyon
Phantom Ranch
Mather Point
Bright Angel
Trailhead
Mather
Campground
South Kaibab
Trailhead
Colorado River
Grand Canyon
National Park
South Rim
N
W
E
S

The Hike
Phantom Ranch
Kaibab Bridge
River Resthouse
Silver Bridge
The Tip Off
Devils Corkscrew
Skeleton Point
Havasupai Garden
Bright Angel Trail
South Kaibab Trail
N
W
E
S
3-Mile Resthouse
1.5-Mile Resthouse
Ooh Aah Point
South Kaibab Trailhead
Bright Angel Trailhead

THE QUEST

Dear Reader,

Thirteen-year-old Jake Evans possesses something valuable: a scrapbook passed down to him by his grandfather, who used it to document his visits to sixty-two United States National Parks.

Inside the scrapbook, his grandfather hid clues, codes, maps, and riddles leading, first Jake, and now his cousin, Wes, and their friend, Amber, on a scavenger hunt through ten national parks.

But the three friends have learned that it's more than a game. For decades, his grandfather had been discovering hidden relics and signs in the national parks. He pieced enough of the clues together to realize he was uncovering an ancient mystery. Knowing he would die before solving the puzzle, he entrusted his quest to Jake.

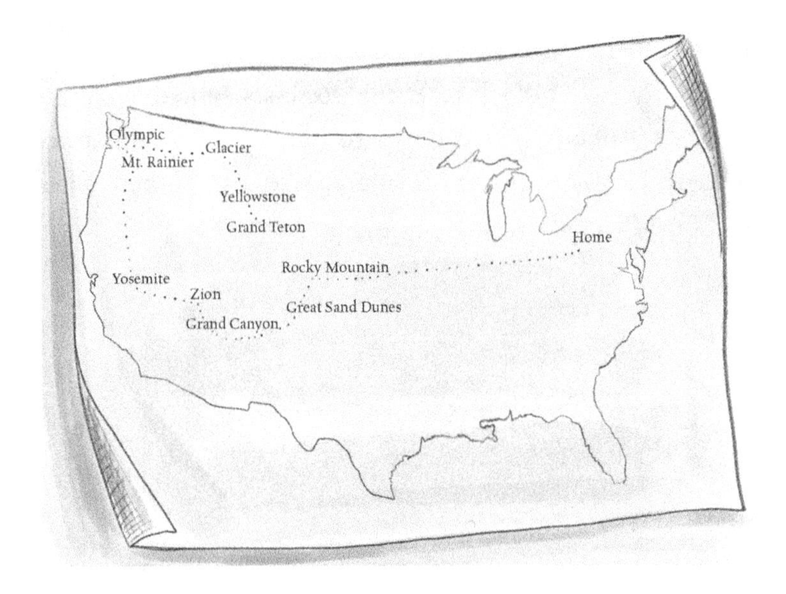

Ten days ago, Jake's family traveled from Ohio to Colorado to begin a two-month vacation in the national parks—a trip his grandfather had planned before his death. In Colorado, at Rocky Mountain National Park, Jake and his friends discovered two important clues. The first came in a package. Inside, he found a heavy, old wooden box and this note:

Burn the package and burn this note. THEY know I have it, and it's no longer safe with me. I'm number 23, which makes you Keeper 24. Here are the instructions I received from 22: You are its steward and protector, charged to keep it hidden. Discover what can be discovered and find the next Keeper. All we've learned has been entrusted to the Marmot.

The box remains locked. There's no keyhole or any other apparent way to open it. A letter from his deceased grandfather instructed Jake to "Keep it locked. You'll find the key in due time."

The second clue they found was a journal, over a century old, containing drawings of an ancient silver spearhead.

They made their next discovery in Great Sand Dunes National Park: a small wooden cube, not much bigger than a golf ball.

By twisting one side of the object, they unlocked the cube, and it unfolded into the shape of a flat cross. Now, as they travel across Utah toward the Grand Canyon, the three friends are trying to understand why Jake's grandpa left this as their next clue.

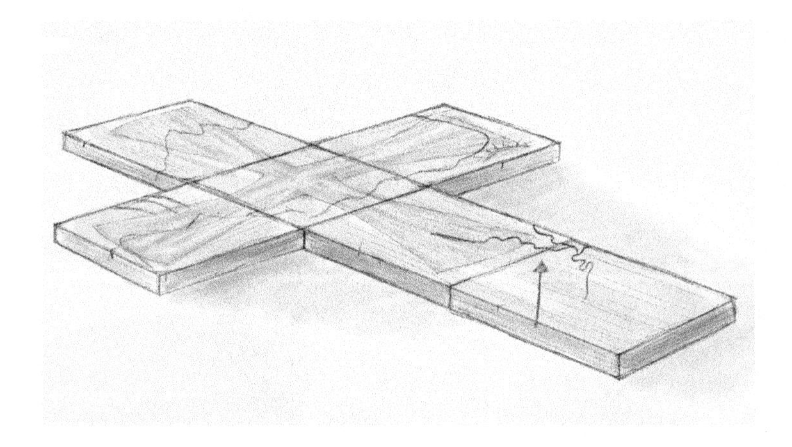

Though Jake has no idea where this adventure will take him, deep in his heart, he understands that it leads to something of great value—because someone else is after it, too. For decades, maybe even more than one hundred years, a shadow group has been on this same quest. The kids have already encountered two suspicious men who they've nicknamed the *Twin Owls*. They've also learned about Owls' boss, a mysterious and powerful figure, known only as the *Director*. The men want the box and the journal. They need the scrapbook and now the cube. And they'll do whatever is necessary to find and take them.

Enjoy the adventure,

Aaron Johnson, Author

Chapter 1

1880 - North Rim of the Grand Canyon

A gunshot echoed off the walls of the canyon. Nahmida startled and crouched low to the ground. Creeping to the edge of the canyon, Nahmida lay on his belly and peered down into the chasm. The sun was in the west, and the shadows made it impossible to see who or what was down there. So, he listened.

He could make out the distant voices of men shouting. He scrambled to his feet, ran along the rim toward the sounds, and then inched out again to listen.

"Boy!" an angry voice yelled. "All we want is that little box. You come out with it, and we leave ya be."

They spoke English. *Haygu*. Outsiders.

Nahmida could see the men now. Their dark suits were covered in the red and gray dust of the canyon. Bowler hats, their rims soaked in sweat, lay upon their heads. And both men trained lever-action rifles on a boulder almost directly below him.

Behind the boulder, he saw a boy, perhaps two years older than himself. His exposed, white skin was baked red from the sun. He had a gash across his forehead, and his arms were abraded. *He must have taken a fall*, Nahmida thought.

"Kid! This is it!" one of the men called out. "You mighta outrun us and outsmarted us, but this is the end of the line. Either you come out with the box, or we put you in one!"

This wasn't right: two grown men hunting a kid as though he was a canyon bear. Nahmida searched for something to trundle over the cliff. If he distracted the men, the boy might have a chance to run. Then a dry, airy rattle filled his ears. He froze.

The rattler's bleached body snaked across the dirt and dust toward Nahmida's face. He didn't move.

"Boy, I'm given ya 'til the count of ten!" The man cocked his rifle. "One...two..."

Ignoring Nahmida, the snake coiled itself tight to bask in the fading sunlight. It tucked its head under its shimmering body.

"Three...four..."

The rattler twitched just inches from Nahmida's face. Its thin pink tongue flickered, then withdrew into the reptile's mouth.

"Five...six...seven..." The man's words ricocheted through the canyon.

In one fell motion, Nahmida's hand shot out and seized the snake by the tail. Springing to his feet, he launched the rattler down toward the men in the canyon below. He watched as its golden body spun through the air.

The men looked up just before the snake landed at their feet. The man who had been counting never made it to eight. He screamed and jumped back. Unharmed by the fall, the snake slithered toward the men, who quickly retreated.

While they were distracted, the boy behind the boulder dashed away and sprinted deeper into the recesses of the canyon. Nahmida knew this place well. There was only one way out, and without his help, the boy would never find it.

Chapter 2

Present Day - Utah

Jake stared at the wooden cube, oblivious to the orange desert landscape outside the window of his aunt and uncle's RV. A dull headache throbbed behind his eyes. Wes's and Amber's nearby voices faded from his awareness. He picked up the cube and carefully twisted one side, unlocking the ancient object. Its sides unfolded on hidden hinges and lay flat on the table, revealing a red Maltese cross. He ran his finger along the golden grooves carved into its wooden surface.

"Miss Elmyra said it was a map," he mumbled to himself. "But how could this be a map?" He recalled the old woman who had given him the cube, her warm smile, and what she had said: "Folks looking for treasure often forget themselves, and they forget what they're really after."

No matter how long he examined it, the five-hundred-year-old artifact refused to reveal its secrets.

I need the scrapbook.

Amber's voice interrupted his pondering. "Jake, come over here and see this."

"Whoa!" Wes said, pressing his face close to the window. "Yeah, Jake, you've got to check this out!"

Jake blinked and looked up from the table. Lit by the sunlight streaming in the window, his cousin's red curly hair blazed like a wildfire. The freckles on Wes's brown skin had darkened during their recent adventures. And like Jake's, the edges of his ears were tinged with sunburn.

Jake steadied himself on the floor of the moving RV. He walked to the small sofa and sat down between Wes and Amber. Outside the tinted window, towers of orange rock vaulted into the sky. Three of the larger columns stood like sentinels guarding an endless desert landscape. Jake felt like he was in a dream, moving from one wondrous scene to the next. He'd hiked in the Rocky Mountains, had just left the Great Sand Dunes, and was now crossing a desert ruled by giant pillars of stone.

Monument Valley

"It's Monument Valley," Wes said. "Those two,"—he pointed out the window—"the ones with the narrow towers on their sides, are called the Mitten Buttes. And that big one there is Merrick Butte."

"It's amazing," Amber breathed. Her caramel-brown hair gleamed in the sunlight. The purple streaks she first arrived with had faded from the sun. "I've seen this place in commercials and movies and stuff, but I had no idea it was this big." She turned to Jake and smiled. "Any luck figuring out the cube?"

He shook his head and grimaced. "No. Nothing." He

sighed. "I'm hoping to find a clue in the scrapbook. When we stop, I can get it from the camper."

As if on cue, the RV slowed, and Jake heard the crunch of gravel under its tires as his uncle turned into a pullout on the side of the road.

"Kids!" his uncle called back from the driver's seat. "We're going to make a quick stop to take pictures."

"Okay, Dad!" Wes shouted back over the rumble of the diesel engine.

"But it's going to be *five* minutes." Uncle Brian held up five fingers. "I want us to get to the campground before dinner. Got it?"

"Got it!" all three kids answered in unison.

As soon as the RV came to a stop, Jake bolted for his family's truck.

"Whoa!" his dad said through the open window. "Let me bring this to a stop first."

Jake bounced on his feet, waiting for his dad to put the truck in park. He hopped the trailer hitch, slid his key into the camper's side door, and went inside. Pulling up the bench to reveal a storage compartment, he pushed his jacket and backpack aside and began rifling through its contents. *There it is!* Jake grabbed the black leather book and raced back to the RV, ignoring his family's photo op.

He settled back into the dining table booth, set the scrapbook on the table, and began turning its pages. The brown paper smelled like burnt vanilla and dust. The scent reminded Jake of his grandfather's attic, where he had found the scrapbook hidden in a secret bookshelf compartment. He flipped past black-and-white photographs of delicate stone arches, Half Dome in Yosemite, and the wildflower-laden meadows of Mount Rainier. Carefully turning each page, he arrived at the Grand Canyon. The old color photographs were like small windows looking out upon a vast wilderness. Muted reds, oranges, and browns showed the colors of the canyon, a jagged layer cake of stone.

The next set of photographs had been taken more recently. Their colors were vibrant. In one of them, his grandpa leaned against a metal railing beside a wooden sign. He held a piece of paper in his hand, and the Grand Canyon filled the space behind him. Jake's eyes lingered on the image of his grandpa.

Amber stepped through the doorway, sat down across from him, and took a drink from her water bottle. "You should get some water in you, Jake," she suggested. "It might help with that headache."

"How'd you know?"

"It's kinda obvious. First, we're in the desert. Second, you're quiet. And third, you've been kinda grumpy." She kicked him playfully under the table.

Jake sighed and glanced around the RV for his blue Nalgene water bottle. "You're right. I'll get some in a bit." He stared at the photograph again. "I just want to figure out this clue."

"So that's him?" Amber leaned forward over the scrapbook. "Your grandpa?"

"Yeah." Jake swallowed and took in a deep breath. Seeing

his grandpa sent a fresh wave of sadness crashing over him, like a homesickness that never goes away.

"He looks happy," Amber added. "And kind."

Wes burst through the door, checking his watch. "Four minutes and forty-three seconds." He slid into the booth beside Amber. "Are you guys checking the backs of the pictures for clues?" he asked.

Jake nodded, then gently pulled the photo of his grandpa out of the triangle photo mounts that had held it to the page. The back was empty. When he pulled a second photo from its mounts, he found something. In faded blue ink, his grandpa had written the letter *P*.

It wasn't the first clue Jake had discovered inside the scrapbook. On his way to Rocky Mountain National Park, he'd found a message scribbled on the back of a photograph. But it had provided instructions. Even the other clues had given him at least a word or two. This was a single letter.

Amber stared down at the letter *P*. "Can we help you check the others?"

"Sure." Jake pulled another photograph from the mounts. On the back, he found a letter *M*.

The photo Amber pulled out had a letter *T* on the back.

Wes's photograph showed the letter *A*. He looked up at Jake with widened eyes. "I bet it spells something!"

Shooting up from his seat like a rocket, Wes pulled a pad of paper and a pencil from the kitchen drawer. When he sat back down, he started writing.

P A M T

"Pamt?" Wes screwed up his face at the sight of the strange word.

"Maybe it's *MAP*?" Amber offered.

"Oh, yeah." Wes wrote *MAP* onto the paper.

"It might be more than one word." Jake flipped a page back to the black-and-white photos. "Maybe the picture of my grandpa, the one with nothing on the back, is supposed to be the space between two words."

He took out another photo, and on its back found the letter *N*.

Wes jotted it down beside the others: *P A M T N.* Then he put down his pencil and helped Jake and Amber remove the rest of the Grand Canyon photos. Counting the one of his grandpa, there were twelve, eleven with letters.

Wes wrote down the remaining letters and pushed the piece of paper to the middle of the table so everyone could see it.

P A M T N I E H O R T

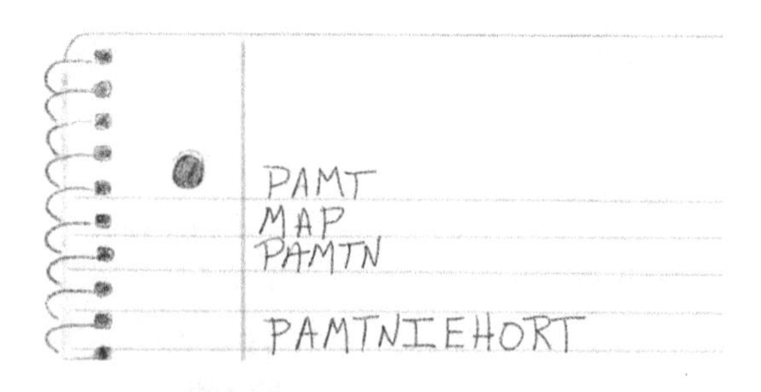

They stared at the letters.

Amber tapped the table. "What if we write each letter on a separate piece of paper? That way, we can rearrange them."

Wes climbed out of his seat again. "Brilliant! I've got sticky notes." He grabbed a small yellow block from the drawer and stuck eleven of them onto the table.

"Okay," Jake said, "let's start with the word *MAP*."

They began moving around the other letters: *T N I E H O R T.*

"Wait, I've got an idea!" Wes pulled a phone from his back pocket. "We can use a word unscrambler."

"They have those?" Jake asked.

"I'm not sure, but I thought I'd check." Wes furiously typed in the search. "Found one! Read me those letters."

Wes plugged the eight remaining letters into the website and hit the *unscramble* button. His face fell. "Nothing." He stared at the screen. "I mean, there are no eight-letter words. The biggest one has seven letters and makes no sense at all."

"Well, read it anyway," Jake said.

"It's *thorite*."

"Thorite map?" Amber wrinkled her brow.

"Like I said," Wes replied, "it makes no sense."

"Are there any other smaller words?" Jake asked.

"Yeah, a bunch, but most of them are more weird words like *ethion*, *hinter*, *tinter*, *norite*, *orient*...."

"*Orient* is a good one," Jake said. "We've got *MAP* and *ORIENT*. What letters are left?"

Amber arranged the sticky notes to spell the words they had. "There are two: *T* and *H*."

Wes slapped the table. "I've got it. It's *ORIENT THE MAP*."

"There's one little problem." Amber tapped the table beside the letter *H*. "There's no letter *E*."

"Maybe Jake's grandpa forgot to write it on the back of the one that's blank." Wes's voice was hopeful as he waited for his cousin to respond.

Jake shook his head. "My grandpa didn't miss details like that. Plug all eleven letters into the unscrambler thing."

Wes put all eleven into the website and hit the *unscramble* button. "There's a bunch of stuff again—none with eleven letters—and a lot of them look like ingredients from the back of a medicine bottle."

"What do you mean?" Amber leaned over to look at the screen.

"Like *atropine*, *ptomaine*, *teraphim*." Wes shrugged. "I can't pronounce half of them."

"But there are some normal words, too," Amber interjected, "like *metaphor*, *patient*, *phantom*...."

Jake clapped his hands together. "That one! That's where we are going tomorrow, *Phantom* something." He collapsed back into his seat, relieved to finally find a word that felt right.

"Yeah." Wes pointed at his cousin. "Phantom Ranch."

"Okay, then what letters are left over after we spell *phantom*?" Amber asked.

They worked together to arrange the stickies to spell *phantom* and set the remaining letters into a group: *I E R T*. Then they began rearranging them and found three new words: *rite*, *tire*, and *tier*.

Jake said them aloud: "*Phantom rite*, *phantom tire*,

phantom tier. None of them make any sense." The hope he'd felt moments ago now felt like a punch in the gut.

"And that's only using the word *phantom* as our starting point," Amber added. "We're just going to have to write out a big list of all the possibilities."

Wes rested his forehead on the table, and in an exasperated voice, said, "That's going to take *hours* to figure out."

"Well, what else are we going to do?" Amber asked.

Jake sat up and leaned in. "Wes, we're going to need a lot more paper."

Chapter 3

1880

Nahmida sprinted along the canyon rim, kicking dust into the light of the setting sun. Pinyon pines flashed by as he ran. His body, not his mind, knew exactly where he was going. He sprang over yucca and rocks, then abruptly stopped, his feet sliding along the gravel and dust.

At his feet was a dark hole just wide enough to slide down. He threaded his legs into the opening, and the gritty sandstone scraped at his sides. As Nahmida climbed down into the narrow slot canyon, the air grew still, and the sounds of the world above him disappeared. He could feel his heart beat against the rock while he squeezed through the passage. Its grip gave way, and he dropped into a small chamber. Overhead, a winding sliver of blue sky ran like a river of fading light.

The chamber opened to a maze of coarse pink and

orange rock. He chose his route, hoping his memory would steer him to the right spot. Ducking into one of the dark tunnels, he sat on his backside and began sliding down a steep and tapered incline. He exhaled and held his breath. Then he pressed his body through another pinch in the rock. The dim light below his feet grew brighter as he sped toward the canyon floor. When his feet finally slammed into solid ground, he immediately crouched to listen. No wind. No voices. Silence. Then came the muted sounds of footfall and labored breathing. The boy was exactly where Nahmida had predicted. Distant cursing followed. The men were closing in.

Nahmida cautiously rounded the corner. The boy was attempting to scramble up the canyon walls and failing miserably. The rock here was brittle and collapsed beneath him as he clawed like a caged animal trying to break free from its captors.

Nahmida whistled a birdcall. The boy turned to face him, his eyes wild with panic.

Nahmida placed a finger to his lips and beckoned the boy to his side. Without a word exchanged between them, the boy followed him through the hidden passage to the small chamber where Nahmida had emerged from the tunnel.

He studied the boy's frame and quickly gripped his torso, then his own, to make certain he would fit. "You'll have to trust me," Nahmida said in English. "This will be tight."

The boy nodded. His cracked lips and dry, shallow breaths worried Nahmida. *Would the boy have the strength to make it?* They had no choice. Nahmida ducked under the alcove and climbed into the cramped tunnel. Behind him, the boy grunted as he, too, pressed himself into the shaft and was enveloped by darkness.

CHAPTER 4

UNSCRAMBLED

The desert landscape outside the RV windows had become flat and barren. Uncle Brian was playing his favorite road trip mix, and *Sweet Home Alabama* was coming through the speakers. Using the unscrambler website, the kids worked for more than an hour, coming up with new word combinations. They started with the longest ones and then unscrambled the leftovers, creating sets of words.

When they exhausted their options, Jake slumped back in his seat again. "It could be *any* of these. I mean, what if the words are some kind of riddle? *Tin metaphor*, *titan morph*, *painter moth*—they all could be another puzzle for us to solve."

Wes dropped his pencil onto the table and sighed. "There are just too many possibilities."

Amber pulled the sheet of paper close and read through all the options, mouthing them silently to herself. Jake picked up the photo of his grandpa, the one picture with no letter on the back.

Why would you make this clue so hard? Jake wondered.

His grandpa stared back at him; his smile seemed to say, "Jax, it's really quite simple."

"Wes," Amber said, still studying the unscrambled words, "how did you figure out the Zapata Falls code at the Sand Dunes yesterday?"

Wes squinted his eyes and wrinkled his forehead. The looter's note had read: *13000604 Fatal Plazas*. It had taken Wes a few days, but he'd cracked the code just in time. It was a word scramble, just like this one, and once decoded, it revealed a time and location.

"I tried to get it into my brain before going to bed." Wes tapped his temple. "That always helps. But it wasn't until we were at the waterfall that it all came together. Like a flash in my mind, I could see that big brown sign with the words *Zapata Falls*."

Jake looked from the photograph to his cousin, and then he sat bolt upright. "Wes, what did you just say?"

"That I figured it out when I saw the sign for Zapata Falls."

Jake looked again at the photograph of his grandpa, then back at Amber and Wes. "Guys, I think I figured out the scramble. And it's not on our list."

"What?" Wes threw his hands up and then grabbed his piece of paper, crumpled it up, and tossed it against the wall. "I don't know if I'm angry or excited." He held his head in his hands. "Maybe I'm...angr...angricited."

Jake didn't have time for his cousin's made-up words. "Look at this." Jake set the photo of his grandpa on the table. "See the sign that's behind him?"

Wes read it out loud, "Mather Point."

Amber started rearranging the sticky notes. The first word came together: *Mather*. Jake held his breath. Five letters remained scattered across the table. Amber set them in order—*P*, and then *O*, *I*, *N*, and finally *T*. Stunned, Jake stared at the words.

Amber beamed. "Nice work, Jake." She leaned back in her seat and folded her arms. "So, what do we do now?"

He had thought that solving the clue would be enough. But he wasn't sure what to do next. Jake shrugged. "I guess...I guess we're supposed to go there." He leaned forward, his elbows on the table. "Remember the first clue in the scrapbook? The one that told me to go to that old cabin in Rocky Mountain National? Maybe that's what this clue is telling us: to go to Mather Point."

Wes rummaged through a storage container at the back of the RV and returned with a book, *Visiting the Grand Canyon*. Thumbing through its pages, he found a map, then set the open book down on the table.

"There it is." He tapped his finger on the dot indicating *Mather Point*.

"Isn't that the name of the campground where we're staying tonight?" Amber asked. "Mather Campground."

"This Mather guy is pretty popular," Wes remarked. "Wait." Wes froze. "Jake, wasn't that the same name as..."

Jake's eyes widened. "The same name that was on the package."

"Really?" Amber asked in disbelief. "The package with the old box in it? The one that you got in Rocky Mountain National Park?"

"And that Mather guy, he wrote you a note," Wes added. "It said something about how he was the Keeper of that box and that now *you* were the new Keeper. And how he said *they* were trying to get it."

Jake scratched his chin. "Exactly. Do you guys remember how my grandpa and his friends used code names? *Mather* is a code name. It stands for the name of one of his friends, the one who sent me the package."

"Makes me wonder who this real Mather is," Wes remarked.

Amber continued to study the map. "So, Mather Point is about a mile-and-a-half from the campground. We could bike there after we get our camp set up. What do you think?"

Jake scanned the items in front of him: the open scrapbook, the sticky notes spelling *Mather Point*, the flattened ancient cube, and Wes's book. He wondered how they might be connected. How would going to Mather Point unravel the meaning of the cube? He didn't know. But he had learned to trust his grandpa's clues by taking the next step. And that thought filled his heart with hope. He looked at Amber and Wes, smiled, and said, "We're going to Mather Point."

Chapter 5

Getting to the Point

They pulled into the campground in the late afternoon. Hikers with trekking poles and hydration packs were returning to their campsites, weary from a long day on the dusty trails along the South Rim. Standing in the middle of their campsite, Jake found it hard to believe that the Grand Canyon even existed. All he could see were pine trees, tents, campers, people, and blue sky.

"Hey, Dad, can we bike to the rim?" Jake asked.

"As long as you're back by dinner." His dad reached into his pocket and pulled out a small blue piece of paper. "You're going to want to add this to your trip." He checked his watch, "But you'll need to leave soon if you want to get there before the post office closes."

Jake took the note from his dad and read:

United States Postal Service. Pick-Up Notice: Certified Mail. Must pick up by June 6th or will be returned to sender.

Grand Canyon Village Post Office. Hours M–F 8:30 a.m. to 5:30 p.m.

"The campground attendant gave that note to me when we checked in," his dad explained. "I bet it's another letter from your grandpa." He smiled.

Jake had received the first letter as he was leaving Rocky Mountain National Park—even though his grandpa passed away six months ago. He'd learned that these were future mail, a way of sending things to be delivered at a future date. "Dad, what time is it?"

His dad looked at his watch. "Five...seventeen."

Jake's face fell. "Can I go?" he stammered. "Like right now."

His dad nodded. "Definitely. Just be aware of cars. This place is busy."

Jake ran to the truck and wrestled his bike out of the bed. Wes, who was helping his dad unfurl the RV's awning, hollered as Jake biked past. "Where are you going?"

"Meet me at Mather Point," Jake called back over his shoulder. "I've got to get something first."

Jake raced off so fast he didn't even think to ask for directions. Seeing the campground office, he swerved into the driveway and rolled up to the window.

An older woman slowly walked up to the counter. The clock on the wall behind her read 5:19.

"Can I help you?"

"Yes," Jake managed to say through heavy breaths. "Can you tell me how to get...to the post office?"

"Of course. I'll be right back," she replied. The attendant took her time to walk across the small room. Jake bit his lip, trying to be patient. His mouth felt dry, so he grabbed the water bottle from its cage on his bike. He was thirsty enough to drink two-day-old water that had baked in the sun, but the bottle was empty.

The woman pulled a pamphlet off a shelf and returned to the counter. "Let me see," she said as she took her time unfolding a visitors map. "Take a right out of the campground. That's Market Plaza Road. Follow that into a big parking lot. The post office will be on your left, just past the general store. You might make it before closing time"—she turned to look at the clock behind her, which now read 5:22, and frowned—"if you hurry."

"Thanks so much." Jake pumped the pedals of his bike and sped out of the campground onto Market Plaza Road. The road ended in a big parking lot full of cars and a long line of them exiting. A sign on a large building read *General Store*, but there was no post office in sight. Then a flagpole and flag caught Jake's attention. He biked toward it. Near the flagpole and hidden behind a cluster of bushy juniper trees, he finally found it.

He rolled onto the sidewalk, leaned his bike against the split rail fence, and sprinted to the door. As he grabbed the handle, he heard a *click* followed by the jangle of keys. A man in a postal uniform looked through the glass door and pointed to a sign that read: *Closes at 5:30 p.m.*

Jake clamped his eyes shut and gritted his teeth. He

wanted to scream. But that felt childish. He couldn't come back in the morning because they'd be on the trail to Phantom Ranch before the post office even opened. He'd miss the letter. It would be returned. And he'd never get the clue.

The postman went through the breezeway and back to the counter. Above him, the clock read 5:28.

Jake rapped on the glass door to get the man's attention. He pointed to the clock, then to his wrist, and back to the clock again. "It's five twenty-eight!"

After glancing at the clock, the postman walked back to the door, unlocked it, and let Jake in.

"Young man, I can help you—if I can do it in sixty seconds."

Jake handed him the blue note, and the man disappeared into the back of the building. He returned and handed Jake a white envelope with a green sticker that read *Certified Mail*. "I'll need you to sign for it." He tapped on the signature screen. Jake signed his name and ripped the envelope open.

"Ahem," the man cleared his throat. "Young man. It really is five-thirty now. We're closed."

"Oh, yeah. Thank you, sir," Jake said as he rushed through the door. Standing beside his bike, he noticed the postmark, November 1st of the previous year—only a few weeks before his grandpa had died. He unfolded the letter to see his grandpa's handwriting. His hands quivered as he held the paper and began reading.

Jake,

I hope you're enjoying the trip and this adventure. The pieces were hidden perhaps by my father or grandfather. Here is what I've been able to figure out so far:

#1 BB Tunnel. Fifteen paces. On your right, you'll need a boost.

#2 Gauging Station, Door 5

#3 Agate at Phantom Ranch

#4 Granary at Indian Garden

With Love,
Grandpa

Jake asked an older couple for directions to Mather Point and was soon biking down a road lined with ponderosa pines and dark green juniper trees. A small herd of elk wandered through the forest only ten yards away. Jake counted four cows along with six spotted calves. They ignored him, set upon some purpose of their own. *Perhaps they're heading for water*, Jake thought. His own mouth was parched. *I hope there's a water fountain at Mather Point.* His thoughts were interrupted by a voice behind him calling out his name.

"Jake! Wait up!"

He looked over his shoulder to see Wes and Amber cranking hard on their mountain bikes to catch up.

"Did you find something?" Wes called out.

Jake stopped his bike alongside the road and pulled out the letter. Amber and Wes brought their bikes to a hard stop, kicking gravel out from under their back tires.

"It's from my grandpa." He unfolded the paper and handed it to Wes. "Another letter he sent using future mail. It's a list of places, but I don't know what it means."

Wes passed it to Amber. "Maybe it'll make sense when we get to Mather Point," Wes offered.

"I hope so." Jake took the letter, folded it, and slid it into his back pocket. "Could I borrow some water from one of you guys?"

"As long as you don't give it back." Amber smirked and handed him her water.

Jake gulped the entire thing down. "Sorry, I was pretty thirsty."

"I can see that," Amber said, taking the empty bottle and sliding it into its cage.

They jumped back on their bikes, and Wes took the lead. Then Amber raced past Jake. He cranked hard, struggling to catch up to her. A touch of frustration rushed through his body, but he pushed it away. His legs were like jelly, and his energy was draining out his toes. He kept pedaling until he was finally able to join them.

"Hey, guys," Wes shouted. "What's bigger than Rhode Island and easy to hide?"

"How could you hide something that big?" Amber asked.

"Look around," Wes answered.

All Jake could see was asphalt, trees, and more trees.

"We're literally at the Grand Canyon, and we can't even see it," Wes half-yelled. "Some of the first explorers totally walked right past it."

"You're not much of an explorer if you walk right past the Grand Canyon," Jake replied.

Wes laughed. "Yeah, but it's easier to miss than you'd think. You can't see it until you're close to the edge."

"I think it's like our clues," Amber said. "They're obvious once we figure them out, but they're easy to miss."

Jake pondered this. She was right. And something inside him felt annoyed with her. *Why was she always right? Not sometimes. Always. And better at everything: biking, running, climbing—everything.*

They rounded a turn and came upon the visitor center complex. Following signs, they biked onto a sidewalk, dismounted, and walked until they found a bike rack. The trio ran down several flights of concrete steps and onto an outcropping that stretched over the canyon. A sign along the rim read *Mather Point.* An instant later, an entire world came into Jake's view. Awed at the sight, the three kids stood at the rim in complete silence.

The westering sun cast an orange glow over hundreds of towering buttes and distant islands of green-brown plateaus. Layer upon layer of redstone rock stretched before them with green trees clinging to the steep canyon walls. Deep blue shadows revealed distant rock formations, like ancient temples carved into the landscape. A yawning and dark chasm tore through the lowest regions, snaking into the hazy distance. It was more than a canyon; it was a canyon full of canyons. There was nothing Jake's mind could conjure that could compare to this, to make sense of its enormity, its shape, or its beauty.

Mather Point

Jake felt his heart expanding, as he tried to become someone who could soak it all in and appreciate the astounding beauty of this place. His grandpa had been that kind of person.

Amber's hushed voice broke the silence. "Can you believe that tomorrow we're going down there? All the way to the bottom."

Jake shook his head slowly in disbelief. *How could there possibly be a trail through such rugged country?* The canyon was an entire world of its own, carved deep into the earth. And they would have only five days down there.

"Wes, what are you doing?" Amber asked.

An island of rock rose above the concrete in the middle of the Mather Point outcrop. Wes was on his hands and knees, pushing and pulling on the stacked stones. "I'm looking for the clue. The only thing around here is this rock. Maybe there's a loose piece with something hidden behind it."

Amber shook her head. "Wes, that's going to take forever."

"Well, I'm committed." He ran his fingers along the seam between two big rocks.

"Guys! I found Mather," Amber called out.

Wes rose to his feet, and both he and Jake ran to Amber's side. Before them was a large granite boulder with a bronze plaque fastened to its surface. Wes read the words out loud:

Stephen Tyng Mather

1867 to 1930

"He laid the foundation of the National Park Service, defining and establishing the policies under which its areas shall be developed and conserved unimpaired for future generations. There will never come an end to the good he has done."

"No wonder his name is on everything around here," Jake said. "He created the National Park Service."

Wes immediately went to work exploring all the cracks and crevices around the boulder. "Maybe the clue is around here somewhere."

Jake leaned against the metal railing and studied the canyon. As the sun slowly descended, shadows revealed the silhouettes of rock formations that had been blurred into the background. The canyon felt alive, like a painting still being created.

"Hey, Jake, look at me," Amber said.

She stood silhouetted by the sunset, holding her camera out in front of her. The faded purple streaks in her hair shimmered in the waning sunlight. She snapped a picture and then walked over and stood beside him. "Check this out." She showed him the picture. "Look familiar?"

Jake's impulse was to ignore her. *I'm trying to figure this out, not waste time taking pictures.* Despite his frustration, he looked at the photo of himself leaning against the rust-colored railing, of the wooden sign, and of the Grand Canyon behind him. It was the exact same spot where his grandpa had been standing in the photograph from the scrapbook.

A lightning bolt of realization shot down his spine. "Guys, I think I just figured it out!"

Wes, still on his hands and knees, looked up from examining a large crack in the gray rock. "You figured out the clue?"

"It's just like you said, Amber. A lot of the clues are *obvious*—once you figure them out."

Wes stood and dusted off his knees. "Okay, but it's not very *obvious* what *you're* talking about right now."

"Remember the picture of my grandpa in the scrapbook? He was right here"—Jake pointed with both of his hands at the ground under his feet—"standing in this *exact* spot at Mather Point!"

Wes shook his head. "I'm not getting it."

"What I mean is that he wasn't telling us to *go to Mather Point*. He was telling us to look at the *photo of him at Mather Point*."

"Ohhhhh," Wes said, before giving Jake a confused look. "But I still don't understand. There was nothing on the back of that photograph. It was blank. There was no clue. Zero. Nada. Nothing."

"It's not what's on the *back*," Jake explained. "I think it's what's on the *front*—something obvious that we missed."

"Like at the sand dunes," Amber said in a hushed voice. "When we shined the flashlight on the photo, it revealed the hidden message."

"Exactly," Jake said.

Wes walked over to join them and crossed his arms in a huff. "You mean we biked all this way here for *nothing*?"

"You're calling *that* 'nothing'?" Amber pointed out toward the Grand Canyon.

Wes turned to see the canyon, now covered in the soft light of the setting sun. "Oh, yeah. I forgot. That's what happens when you're on your knees staring at rocks."

"The clues always go back to the scrapbook," Amber said. "We can't forget that."

"You're right, Amber." It escaped his lips, and he wanted to take it back. But she was right; the scrapbook was their guide and source of their clues.

Their adventure would begin at sunrise. Jake's chest churned with nervous anticipation. But he had to figure this clue out tonight, and that meant getting the photograph of his grandpa at Mather Point. Jake turned to leave, wanting to race back and find the photo, but he was stopped in his tracks, captured by the sunset.

All three kids watched as shadows crept across the

canyon. Yellows became orange, and oranges became vermil-
lion. The canyon's depths darkened, and its rim was set
ablaze with the last rays of sunlight.

Chapter 6

To Build A Fire

Jake, Amber, and Wes raced back to the campground in the fading light of the setting sun. Jake dropped his bike, and it clattered to the ground as he sprinted for the camper door.

"Is that how we treat our things?" Jake's dad stood beside his bike, his hands on his hips.

"Sorry, Dad." Jake picked it up and gently leaned it against the tongue of the trailer hitch.

"Not sure what you've got planned, but it'll have to wait till after dinner." His dad put his hand on Jake's shoulder. "And I hate to be the one to break the news, but you're on dish duty tonight."

Jake's shoulders drooped.

Night crept across the sky during dinner, and a chill set in. Orange campfires sprang up in the dark blue distance. A cloud of smoke wafted into their site.

Wes coughed. "Why do fires have to be so smoky?"

"They don't have to be," Uncle Brian answered. "It's all about how you build it."

"Can you show us how?" Jake asked.

"Sure thing. After dinner...and dishes," his uncle replied.

Dang it. He'd added yet another activity before he could examine the photograph. Dinner, then dishes, and now building a fire. Amber seemed to recognize this, too, because she glared at him from across the picnic table.

The three kids wolfed down their dinner. Wes pitched in by taking plates and silverware from the parents. Jake washed, and Amber dried the dishes. Jake's leg muscles tightened and twitched. Something wasn't right. He didn't feel sick. Not yet, anyway. But his body felt weak and strange.

They finished the dishes in a flash. "Now's our chance." The three kids ran to the camper, and Jake pulled out the picture of his grandpa from the scrapbook.

"Amber, can you shine your flashlight on it?" he asked.

She cast the light across the glossy paper of the photo, but there was no hidden writing like there had been on the vista of the Great Sand Dunes.

Then Jake saw something. He had been so drawn to the image of his grandpa and his magnetic smile, he'd missed what was in his grandpa's *hands*: a piece of paper with a drawing on it—something that looked familiar.

"No way!" Jake blinked his eyes and then looked more closely at the image.

"It's the..." Amber began.

"It's the...cube," Jake said. "I mean, it's a *drawing* of the cube after it's open and flat. See the Maltese cross. And there are more lines and writing."

"Can you make it out?" Amber asked.

"Yeah, it looks like it says, 'Find the missing...'"

"Find the missing *what*?" Wes bounced up and down on the balls of his feet.

"I can't make out the rest," Jake answered. "We'll need some way to..."

They were interrupted by Uncle Brian, who peered in the camper door. "Hey, kids, it's fire time."

Jake carefully tucked the photo into his jacket pocket. "We'll figure it out tonight. I promise."

Outside, Uncle Brian set a battery-powered camp lantern on the ground near the fire ring. The light revealed the red color of his beard and camo pattern of his long-sleeve shirt.

"First things first," he began. "Are we even allowed to *have* a fire?"

Wes looked around at the other campsites. "Well, everybody has one."

"Wrong answer," Uncle Brian replied. "Wes, you know this."

"Oh, yeah, we've first got to check and see if there's a fire ban."

"Explain that to everybody else." Everyone, even the other parents, leaned forward to listen. Uncle Brian had been a survivalist trainer in the Army. His stories and lessons captured everyone's attention. But this time, it was Wes's turn.

"Well, the forest service, or rangers, has to decide whether it's too dry and dangerous for a fire. That's how a lot of wildfires get started—from campfires. So, if it is too dry, they declare a fire ban."

Uncle Brian patted his son on the back. "I checked with the campground office, and there's no ban right now. But all fires have to be made and kept inside these metal rings." He tapped the ring with the toe of his boot. "And I've filled a five-gallon bucket with water." Lifting the lantern, he cast its glow upon an orange plastic bucket. "If the fire were to get out of control, we've got a way to put it out. And we'll use it to extinguish the fire before we turn in for the night." His expression was serious. "All right, kids, next question: What are the three key ingredients to a good fire?"

"Well, there's fuel," Jake answered. "You've got to have sticks and logs and stuff."

"And you need a spark, some way to start the fire," Amber added.

"Good," Uncle Brian replied. "You need fuel and spark, but there's one more thing most people neglect. And they forget because they can't *see* it."

All three kids scrunched up their faces.

"But you can *feel* it," Uncle Brian added.

"You can't *see* it, but you can *feel* it?" Jake repeated. "Could you give us another clue?"

Uncle Brian smiled. "Sure. You need this to survive, and so does a fire."

"Can't see it. Can feel it. Can't live without it," Wes said, "I like this. It's like a riddle." He rubbed his hands together. "And we're good at riddles. Let's crack this thing!"

Jake's brain felt foggy. "Maybe just one more clue?" he asked.

Uncle Brian didn't answer. Instead, he started whistling. It was perhaps the worst attempt at whistling Jake had ever heard.

"That's it!" Amber pointed at Uncle Brian. "It's air! It's *oxygen*. You can feel it, but you can't see it, and you can't live without it."

"Exactly!" Uncle Brian gave her a high five.

A cold tinge of jealousy crept over Jake's shoulders. *How does Amber always figure things out so fast?* He swept the thought away and slid his hands into his pockets to keep them warm. His fingers found the contours of the photograph, and his breathing quickened. He leaned in, trying to pay attention to his uncle.

He pulled some sprigs of grass from the ground and gently tossed them into the air. "What am I doing?" He picked some more grass and tossed it again.

"I know," Amber tucked a loose strand of hair over her ear. "You're finding what direction the wind is blowing."

Jake was annoyed. *Seriously, how does she always do that? I could have figured it out if I had one more second.*

"Exactly!" Uncle Brian crouched down close to the fire ring. "We want to funnel that air into the fire." He removed the remains of a charred log from the ashes. "And we don't want something like this blocking it." Using his camp shovel, he scraped away the gray and black mess to unclog them. "This will help the oxygen get under the fire."

After picking some paper out of the camp trash bag, he

crumpled it up. "This is tinder. It goes at the bottom of the fire to get things started."

"But, Dad," Wes interjected, "what if we're out in the woods and don't have any paper?"

"Think about it." Uncle Brian tapped his brow. "What might burn easily?"

"Maybe dead grass and leaves," Jake offered.

"Bingo!" Uncle Brian gave him a fist bump. Getting something right helped a little to lessen the grudge that had been growing. *I shouldn't be upset with Amber*, he thought. *It's not like this is a competition.*

"Now, I've got a favorite thing," his uncle continued, "that I use for tinder when I'm out in the woods, something called *old man's beard.*" He stroked the curly red hair along his chin. All three kids looked at him like he was crazy.

Wes asked the question they were all thinking, "You use your beard hair to start fires?"

Uncle Brian laughed. "No, don't be silly. Beard hair has too much moisture in it." He winked at the kids. "Old man's beard is a kind of lichen, a green moss-looking thing that grows on spruce trees. You ball that stuff up, and it's perfect for getting your fire going." He rested his hands on his hips. "Okay, we've got our tinder; what do you think is next?"

"Kindling," Wes half-shouted. "All the small sticks and stuff."

"Correct." Uncle Brian gave his son a proud smile. "Wes, earlier you asked why fires had to be so smoky. Most of the time, it's because people put thick logs on their fire without enough kindling to get the fire superhot." He pulled small strips of firewood from under the picnic table and set them on the ground.

Jake, Amber, and Wes each grabbed a handful of kindling. Uncle Brian showed them how to build a log cabin fire structure for their fire that would leave plenty of room for oxygen.

Uncle Brian looked across the fire ring to Amber. "Do you want to light it?"

She smiled and nodded, and he tossed her the box of matches.

Disappointment settled on Jake like a wet blanket. He wanted to start the fire.

Amber struck a match and gently touched it to the paper. Everyone watched as the small blue flame crept up through the cardboard and caught the smallest slivers of kindling on fire. The flame grew and crackled as it consumed more of the wood.

Uncle Brian clapped his hands together. "Perfect. Now we can lay some bigger pieces of kindling across the top."

The boys grabbed the wood and set them carefully over the growing fire. When it had grown hot enough, they did the same with three small logs. The fire flickered and popped.

"Well done, kids," Uncle Brian said. "The key ingredients are tinder, kindling, oxygen, and...*patience*." He settled into his camp chair. "And our hike these next five days is going to test that."

"Our fire-building skills?" Wes asked, sounding confused.

Uncle Brian smiled at his son. "Patience. A demanding

hike like this one is going to put some strains on you. And patience with one another is going to be your glue."

Jake fingered the edges of the photograph again. Patience was the last thing he wanted to hear about right now.

"Well," Jake's dad interjected, "it's getting late, and we *are* hitting the trail at six o'clock. So, we oughta all get to bed."

Jake's heart dropped. "Dad, can we have, like, fifteen minutes? There's something we *have* to do before bed—something that Grandpa left for me—and we have to figure it out...*tonight.*"

Mr. Evans nodded and smiled. "Sure thing. But make it quick. You guys need your rest."

Chapter 7

The Photograph

Inside the camper, the three kids slid into the bench seats at the dining table.

Amber leaned in with a concerned look on her face. "Are you okay, Jake? You don't look like yourself."

"I think I'm just tired." He pulled the photograph out of his pocket.

"Can I see it again?" Wes asked.

Jake handed the photograph across the table. Wes held it close to his eyes, trying to make out the rest of the sentence.

"'Find the missing...'" He paused. "You're right, Jake. It's totally impossible to read."

"Do you have a magnifying glass or something in your RV?" Jake asked.

"Why would I have a magnifying glass?" Wes ran his fingers through the tight red curls of his hair.

Both Jake and Amber stared at him, their eyebrows raised. Then Amber said exactly what Jake was thinking.

"Because you seem to have *everything* in there." She grinned. "It's like a warehouse on wheels."

Wes pursed his lips and nodded. "That's fair. I've pretty much got everything we need in there—except a magnifying glass. But, you've got one." He gently elbowed Amber.

"Me?" Amber pointed with her thumb at herself.

"Yeah, just use your phone to take a photo of it and zoom in on it."

Amber hit her forehead with the palm of her hand. "How did we not think of that?"

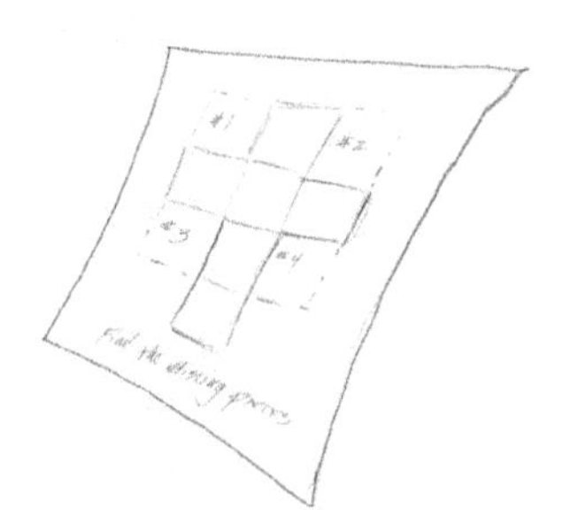

"Well, *I* thought of it," Wes said under his breath.

He set the photograph on the gray-speckled surface of the table. The camera on Amber's phone clicked, and she zoomed in on the words. Jake leaned in to see and bumped his head against hers. "Sorry." He drew back a few inches.

Amber squinted and rubbed her forehead.

"You okay?" he asked.

"I'm totally fine," she replied, still staring at her phone, the light illuminating her face.

"Can you read it?" Wes asked.

"I can. It says: 'Find...the...missing ...*pieces*.'" She paused and then moved the photo on the screen. "But there's more —not more words—but more to the drawing." She passed the phone to Jake. "It looks like numbers."

Wes shot out of his seat. "I'll be back. I'm getting my sketchpad."

He was back in a flash with the pad and pencil.

"Can I see the photo?" Wes asked.

Jake slid the phone across the table, and Wes zoomed in on the different parts of the photo, copying it onto the paper.

"Here it is, guys." Wes pushed the phone back to Amber and set the drawing in the center of the table.

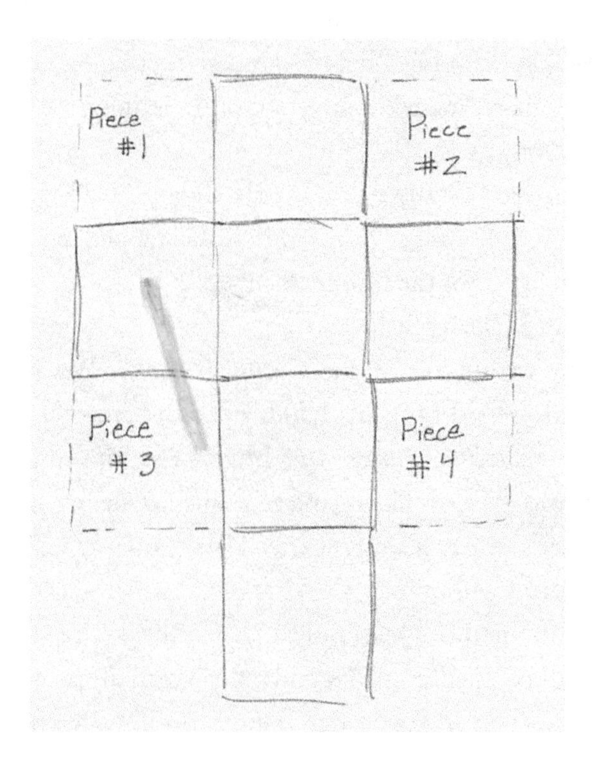

Wes's drawing was an exact copy of the paper Jake's grandpa had been holding in the photograph. In the middle was the cross shape of the wooden cube. At its corners were dotted lines indicating four missing squares.

Jake opened the bench seat compartment, brought out the cube, unlocked it, and laid it open on the table.

The kids gazed at the flattened cube and the drawing in stunned silence.

Jake looked back up at Wes and Amber. "So...our mission," he said in a hushed voice, "is to find the missing pieces and complete the map."

Wes's eyes got big. "Let me get this straight: there are four missing squares made out of wood or something."

Jake nodded.

"And each of those square tile thingies is like...like *two square inches*." Wes's voice rose as he tapped one of the missing corners of the unfolded cube.

"Yeah," Jake replied.

"But we are like at the *Grand Canyon*!" Wes breathed hard and pressed both his hands onto the table. "It's huge! Like *two thousand square miles* huge!" He gripped the sides of his head. "That's like trying to find a needle in a haystack. No, no, it's worse. It's way worse. There's no way we're going to find them without..."

"Without this!" Jake pulled the certified letter from his back pocket. He unfolded it and set it beside the drawing.

"One, two, three, four." Jake tapped on each of the missing pieces at the corners of the cross. Then he ran his finger along the list in the letter. "Four missing pieces—and four clues."

Wes stared at his cousin with his mouth agape. "Your grandpa was a genius!"

"And our first clue," Amber breathed, "is hidden in a tunnel."

Jake folded the letter, then the cube. "We've got our mission, guys. Let's do this."

He placed his fist in the middle of the table. Amber stacked her fist on top of Jake's.

Wes looked at them and said, "Is this like our secret-team-hand-stack thingy?"

Jake grinned. "I guess."

"I think it would work better if we just stacked hands," Wes remarked.

Jake and Amber flattened their fists into open hands.

"Wait!" Wes exclaimed. "That's perfect! It's just like the cube, how it's three-dimensional, then it goes flat. What if we start with stacked fists, count to three, then flatten them out."

Amber snickered. "Wes, you crack me up. But I like it."

The three kids stacked their fists and looked at one another. They counted to three and let their fists drop into a hand stack.

"Oh, that was definitely cool," Wes said.

Amber and Jake laughed.

"Can we keep it?" Wes asked, a sheepish look on his face.

Jake and Amber answered at the same time with the same word. "Definitely."

Chapter 8

1880

Nahmida pressed his feet and fingers into the sides of the steep passage, pushing himself to the top. He emerged from the hole like a badger scrambling out of its burrow. Laying on his belly, he stretched an arm back into the tunnel to pull the boy out. Moments later, the boy sat beside Nahmida in the dust, chest heaving. Nahmida could see relief and gratitude in his eyes.

"Where is your horse?" Nahmida asked.

The boy appeared surprised by the question.

Nahmida asked again. "Do we need to return for your horse?"

"How," the boy stammered, "did you know... I have a horse?"

"You smell like horse sweat," he pointed to the tunnel opening. "I was afraid a horse had joined us in there." A smile crept across Nahmida's face.

The boy let out a tired snicker and wiped the sweaty grit

from his brow. "I left the horse with a farmer—about a day's journey from here." His eyes narrowed as if suddenly confused. "How do you know English?"

"I will tell you later." Nahmida got to his feet and dusted off his knees. "We must first get you water and find a safe place to rest."

The boy stretched out his hand, and Nahmida drew him to his feet. Still holding onto his hand, the boy said, "My name is Abe. Thanks for saving me."

"You're welcome, Abe. My name is Nahmida."

The boys scrambled out of the slot canyon and back to the high canyon rim, where Nahmida found a game trail used by bighorn and deer. He pointed at the trail and then down into the canyon, "This one leads to water, see."

A hint of green was visible below them, but the path to it was indiscernible. The sky was a darker blue, and the first stars were appearing in the east. Abe stumbled along, stopping often to catch his breath as they made their way along the sheer canyon wall, over loose rock, and further down into the great chasm.

An hour later, the trickling sounds of water filled their ears. The cacti at their feet gave way to softer and greener plants. Nahmida yearned for the water, and he could only imagine how Abe felt. Rounding a tall column of red sandstone, a thin horsetail waterfall came into view. Pouring from a fissure in the canyon wall, the water cascaded down a long ramp of moss-covered and glistening pink rock till it crossed the game trail at their feet. Hoofprints were scattered about the soft earth surrounding the water.

Abe fell to his knees and began to draw water from the pool. Nahmida placed his hand on Abe's back. "Go slowly, my friend, or you will make yourself sick."

Abe exhaled and nodded. "Thank you."

Nahmida made his way into a copse of willow trees and then to the canyon wall. Along its red rock surface, he found a gritty white substance. After scraping some of it into the palm of his hand, he returned to Abe. "Mix this with some water to make a paste," Nahmida said, dropping the soft grains into Abe's hand. "Then put it in your mouth before you drink again."

Abe put a pinch of it on his tongue. "Salt?"

Nahmida nodded. "It will help."

After Abe followed his instructions, Nahmida drank from the pool and then sat down. "We will need food and a warm place to sleep." He gestured to the path they had taken to the spring. "When you are ready, we must return to the plateau."

Abe's brow wrinkled as he stared up at the high canyon walls. "I think I have the strength now. But the men—I'm certain they will search for me there."

Nahmida's eyes scanned the darkening sky as he thought through their options. "They will search for you. But they will never find you—not where we're going."

Chapter 9

The South Kaibab Trail

Jake's eyes blinked open at 5 a.m., and a rush of anticipation flooded his body, followed by a dull ache behind his eyes. Today they would hike into the heart of the Grand Canyon. He rubbed his forehead in hopes it might help the headache. *Maybe I didn't drink enough water yesterday.* He unzipped his sleeping bag, grabbed his water bottle, and guzzled as much as his stomach could hold.

Slinging his backpack over his shoulder, Jake plunged out the door. But when his feet hit the ground, he remembered something. He went back inside the camper, opened the compartment, grabbed the cube, and stuffed it into the top of his pack.

They drove to the shuttle stop where Jake stood in the chill of the early morning. Wes and Amber stood beside him in silence as they waited in the dark for the shuttle to arrive. The parents were more talkative than the groggy kids.

Uncle Brian greeted them. "Hey, sleepy heads."

Wes grunted at his dad, and Amber lifted her eyes to give Uncle Brian her attention.

"So, I know you guys would like to do this hike down to Phantom Ranch on your own. That's fine. Just stay on the South Kaibab Trail. It's pretty much the only trail, so that won't be difficult." He gave the bill of Jake's ball cap a playful tap.

Jake adjusted his hat and nodded. "Okay. What if the parents go ahead of us, and the three of us hike as a group? We promise not to fall too far behind."

"That works," Uncle Brian replied.

"How long will it take to get down there?" Wes asked.

"It's seven miles—and all downhill, of course." Uncle Brian handed Amber a folded topo map. "We're getting an early start, so I'm thinking we'll arrive at Phantom Ranch sometime before lunch."

Just then, the shuttle pulled up, and the three families climbed inside. The slightest hints of dawn cast a red line across the horizon in the east. At the South Kaibab Trailhead, the parents gave their kids hugs before they departed.

Hiking backward, Uncle Brian asked, "What are the three most important things to remember?"

Wes pulled on the hose of his hydration pack and answered, "Water, water, and...water."

His dad smiled and then looked each of them in the eyes. "We trust you three." Then he turned and followed the other parents who had already started down the trail. "See you at the bottom!" he called back.

As Jake watched the parents disappear below the canyon

rim, the sun broke the horizon and cast its rays across the landscape. It was as if someone had turned on a light bulb in a dim room. The yellows and oranges of last night's sunset were replaced with soft purples and blues.

Amber had unfolded the map. "So, what are we looking for again?"

Jake had memorized all four clues. "The first one said: *BB Tunnel. Fifteen paces. On your right, you'll need a boost.*"

"We follow the South Kaibab Trail all the way to the bottom." Her finger traced the trail. "But there's no tunnel marked anywhere on here." Jake walked over to study the map with her.

Wes scrunched up his face. "How about the *BB* part?"

Amber began noting the landmarks along their trail. "There's Ooh Ahh Point and Skeleton Point, and then something called The Tip Off..."

"What about that?" Jake set his finger on the spot where the trail crossed the Colorado River.

Amber held the map closer to her eyes to make out the tiny writing. "It says...Black...Bridge."

"That's it!" Wes clapped his hands together. "*BB*, Black Bridge."

Amber didn't look convinced. "But still, there's nothing on here about a tunnel." She rubbed her chin. "I guess we'll have to figure things out when we get there." She looked at Jake, her brow furrowed with concern. "Are you okay? You keep holding your head."

Jake shrugged. "Just a headache."

"Okay," she replied, folding the map. "Wes, can you put

this in the back of my pack?" She handed it to him and turned to face Jake again. "Let us know if we need to slow down or something. There's no rush. We can take it easy."

Annoyed by her comment and frustrated by the dull throbbing behind his eyes, Jake huffed, "I'm okay. I don't need special treatment."

And with one step, they began their journey into one of the most beautiful and demanding places on earth. The trail hugged the side of the canyon as it zig-zagged through the landscape. After a few minutes of hiking, Jake could feel his lungs working, and the pressure behind his forehead began to subside. His legs and knees still felt weak, but he had the strength to lift his head and take in the sunrise. Below them, a red rock formation rose into the air like an ancient temple. The morning light illuminated flat tablelands of sage green that fell away into dark and chiseled side canyons.

Like yesterday's bike ride, Jake had a hard time keeping

up with Amber and Wes. He could hear them talking but was too far behind to make out any of the details of their conversation. Eventually, they stopped at a sign on the edge of a long outcrop, and Jake was able to catch up to them.

"You doing okay, Jake?" Wes asked.

"I'm fine," he murmured.

"You can use my trekking poles if you want." Wes stretched his poles out toward his cousin.

"No thanks." Jake's legs felt wobbly and weak. *I'm okay. It'll get better.* He sipped some water in hopes that it might help.

"We're at Ooh Ahh Point." Amber looked at the map. "That means we've gone about a mile."

Wes had walked out onto the gray stone of the outcrop. "Oooooooh," he said, looking down into the canyon. "Ahhhhhhhhhhhh." He pinched his chin and slowly nodded his head. "Appropriately named."

Though Jake wasn't feeling well, he had to grin at his cousin's silliness. Jake decided to take the lead. "Come on, guys, let's keep moving."

The trail turned into hundreds of stairs winding through the red sandstone. Amber and Wes stayed on Jake's heels, talking as they hiked. This was so different from their adventures in the high altitudes of Rocky Mountain National Park. It was so much easier to breathe here.

"This place is like a geologist's dream!" Wes said. "I mean, you can see all the different layers of rocks."

The heat from the rising sun chased the cool of the morning away. When they reached Skeleton Point, the three kids took off their packs and relaxed in the shade of a small shelter.

"Wes, you packed the drawing of the cube, right?"

"Uh-huh." Wes pulled out the drawing of the cube and the four missing pieces he had made the previous night. "Here it is." He handed it to Jake.

"Thanks." Jake winced, and he rubbed his forehead before studying the paper. "Elmyra Holcomb said the cube was a *map*."

Amber leaned over to study it. "A map of the Grand Canyon?"

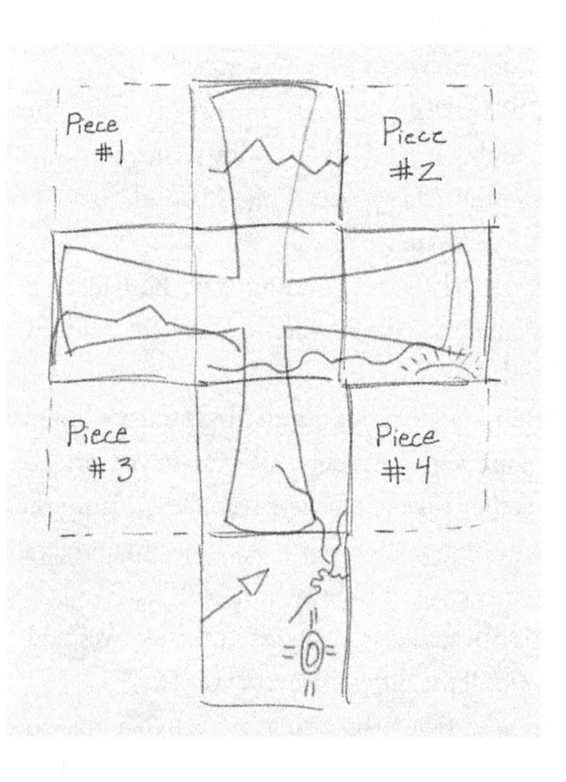

"That's what I'm wondering," Jake said, examining the cube's markings that Wes had copied onto the paper. "This looks like a river." His finger traced a long line that curved through the drawing.

"Yeah, it does," Amber replied. She looked out to the landscape below them, then back at Wes's drawing. "I can't see anything that matches it."

"Me either." Jake handed the paper back to Wes.

Wes stood up, and like Jake and Amber, tried to see if anything in his drawing matched the landscape. Eventually, he gave up, sat back down, and began eating some beef jerky. But he kept looking over his shoulder at a bench where an older couple sat talking. Both had gray hair, looked athletic for their age, and were dressed in hiking gear. The man had a huge camera with a telephoto lens. By the size of their packs, they probably had a tent and sleeping bags for an overnight trip.

Amber elbowed Wes. "Why do you keep looking over at those people?"

Wes leaned in and whispered, "They're suspicious."

Amber laughed. "Why would you say that? Look at them; they're cute. When I'm that age, I want to be active and hiking like they are."

"They may be cute," Wes replied, "but they've been behind us for the entire trip—and they stop whenever we do."

"What other choice do they have, Wes?" Jake said. "There's only one trail, and they're stopping to rest like everyone else." He gestured to the other hikers who were sitting in the shade of the resthouse structure.

"Still, I've got a funny feeling." Wes glanced back at the couple again. "I'm going to keep an eye on them."

Amber rolled her eyes and shouldered her pack. "We should get going."

Chapter 10

The Heat

They continued their hike down into the broad, green tableland they had seen from the top, the Tonto Plateau. But to get there, the kids had to traverse a series of winding, steep switchbacks that looked more like the rails of a roller coaster than a hiking trail.

A half-hour later, they were trekking across the broad, open plain of the Tonto Plateau. Without the occasional shade cast by the canyon walls, the heat of the sun began sapping their strength. Jake's back ached, and the headache surged again. Sweat dripped down his brow and stung his eyes.

At their next stop, a place called The Tip Off, they ate snacks and reapplied sunscreen. Jake sat down on a small boulder and guzzled more water.

"Jake, you don't look good," Amber said.

He was too fatigued to protest as he had earlier. Instead, he nodded slowly and bent down to retie his bootlaces.

Stairs to the Tonto Plateau

Wes, who was reading a trail sign, called back, "Maybe you've got heatstroke."

"Whatever it is...it doesn't feel good," Jake admitted.

"The sign says the symptoms are slurred speech, irritability, confusion, and a super high temperature," Wes explained.

"You have been pretty grumpy," Amber remarked. "And you didn't drink much water yesterday. Remember, you left your water bottle in the truck during the drive."

Jake didn't like Amber telling him what he already knew. "Being grumpy doesn't mean I've got heatstroke." His voice was terse.

"The sign says there's something called *heat exhaustion*. It's not as bad, but it's still pretty serious." Wes read the symptoms out loud. "Headache, dizziness, fatigue, clammy skin, and heavy sweating."

Jake held his head in his hands and mumbled, "Check, check, check, check, and check. I've got all of those."

"Well, we need to go slow then," Amber said. "And rest in the shade when we find some."

Wes handed Jake his trekking poles. "And take these. They'll help."

"Thanks, guys." His words were sluggish. "I'm sorry I'm slowing us down."

"We aren't in any rush," Amber said. "Remember what Wes's dad said last night about patience?"

"It's our glue—what holds us together," Wes said.

Using the trekking poles for support, Jake stood to his feet. A wave of nausea ran from his gut up to his throat.

Wes continued to jabber. "I was reading this story about some explorers in Antarctica whose boat got frozen in the ice. They were lost and stranded for almost *two years*. But every one of them survived because their leader always went at the speed of the slowest person."

The words "slowest person" irritated Jake. Wes was definitely referring to him. And Jake took it personally. *I'm not slow. I just don't feel well.* He decided not to say anything. He didn't want to snap and look stupid.

"That's pretty smart," Amber commented. "Patience like that can save your life."

Jake's foggy brain was making it hard to hear anything

beyond his own thoughts, the crunch of his boots on the trail, and the rap and tap of the trekking poles each time they hit the ground. His mood continued to sour like milk left out in the sun.

Amber shaded her eyes and looked down into the canyon below. "Is that a river?"

Wes stopped and pulled out his binoculars. "Sure is." He handed them to her.

Jake leaned on the poles and stared until he could just make out a thin emerald-colored channel threading its way through the bottom of the canyon. Amber handed him the binoculars. With them, he could see a brown sandbar and the white riffles of rapids at its edges. It felt so far away. Being this close should have encouraged him, but Jake didn't know if he could make it.

"That's got to be the Colorado River," Amber remarked. "Didn't a ranger in Colorado tell us that the river starts as melted snow in Rocky Mountain National Park?"

"Yep. That's what the ranger said," Wes replied. "Looks like the river followed us all the way here to Arizona."

Amber shook her head at Wes's attempt to be silly, then gently grabbed Jake's elbow. "Jake, why don't we stop here for a few minutes since we have a bit of shade?"

Jake shook off her hand, muttered an "uh-huh" and leaned against the rock wall beside him. Its smooth surface was still cool from the long night. The chill soaked into his hot skin. Eyes closed, he could tell Amber and Wes were both staring at him with concern. His breaths were shallow and strained. He'd never felt like this before. *Maybe if I can just rest.* He rested his head against the rock.

"Hey, Jake." Amber's voice sounded far away. "Jake." He felt her gently shake his shoulder. "Jake, you've got to wake up."

Then he heard Wes. "Do you think we should go get help?"

He snapped awake. "How...how long was I out?"

"Just a few minutes." Amber's face was as serious as the stone walls behind them.

"I'm ready," Jake mumbled. He took a slow set of steps forward. "I'll lead out."

The trail snaked like a pink and orange serpent down a long, steep gully. Soon, the path crested a dark, jagged outcrop that loomed above the river. A metal suspension bridge spanned its green and silent waters. Seeing the water inspired Jake to hike faster, but his body could not. Wes and Amber whispered as they walked. And his frustration grew.

Jake halted and turned to face them. "Stop it!" A dam of anger burst. "Stop whispering. And stop acting like I'm a problem. I'm not."

"Jake, we're not upset with you," Amber said. "We're just kinda scared, and we're trying to figure out how to help you. And Wes was just saying..." She turned to Wes, who was still stunned and silent from Jake's outburst.

"I was just saying that the older couple"—he pointed up the trail to where the silhouettes of two hikers stood—"keep stopping every time we stop. It's a little weird."

Jake ignored his cousin. He hated how his mind roiled

and that he couldn't shut it off. Regret swirled with anger, but he couldn't form the words to say sorry. Instead, he shook his head in frustration, turned, and continued trudging down the trail.

As they rounded another switchback, the distant murmur of flowing water filled Jake's ears. The thrum grew louder with each step. He could now see the ripples in the water and hikers crossing the bridge. As the trail curved into the shadow of the craggy outcrop, the water sounds ceased. They found themselves in a corridor of stone, a long hallway of chiseled rock. At the end of the passage gaped the dark mouth of a tunnel.

Chapter 11

Into the Tunnel

"No way," Wes's voice breathed from behind Jake. "*This* has got to be it."

Jake didn't speak. *I should feel excited, but all I want to do is find a bed or throw up, anything that would help me feel better.* He forced himself to step into the long, dark tunnel. The floor was covered with fine dust and the boot prints of other hikers. The jagged walls had been chipped away in giant chunks by whoever carved this place out of the side of the canyon. From the opposite end of the tunnel, a yellow-orange light cast a dim glow through the space. The sounds of the river, along with a cool breeze, pulsed along the tunnel walls.

Jake leaned against the rock, pulled the paper from his pocket, and read the clue: *#1 BB Tunnel. Fifteen paces. On your right, you'll need a boost.*

Amber stood at the entrance. "I can pace it out. Fifteen, right?"

"Yeah, it's fifteen paces," Jake muttered. *Maybe I can save my strength for finding the clue.*

"Thirteen, fourteen, fifteen." Amber stopped just beyond where Jake stood. "So, it should be somewhere up there?" She pointed above their heads and to the right.

Jake laid the trekking poles on the ground. Heatstroke or no heatstroke, he was going to scale the wall. His fingers struggled in vain to grip the rock. He tried cramming his foot into a gap, pressing with all his might. It wasn't enough. His foot slipped. His knee smashed into a rock. His head hit the wall, and he fell backward into the dirt.

Amber rushed to his side. "Are you okay?" She reached out her hand. Jake took it and slowly got to his feet.

She examined the scrape on his forehead. "You're going to have a mean bruise."

Jake squeezed his eyes shut and let out a long sigh. Just when he thought he couldn't feel worse, he'd gone and slammed his head into a rock wall. Bending over, he rolled up the leg of his hiking pants to reveal his bloodied knee.

Wes cringed. "That looks like it hurts."

It did. The throbbing of Jake's knee competed with the throbbing in his head.

"What if we help?" Amber offered. "Your grandpa's note said you'd need a boost."

"Okay," he exhaled. "Let's try."

Wes and Amber wove their fingers together and placed them under Jake's feet. He could feel Wes struggling to steady himself. Jake's shakiness and exhaustion conspired to throw him off balance. The tunnel began to spin. Grappling with the rock, his hands were too weak to grip.

"You guys...I can't...do it," he stammered. "Just...just...put me down." Amber and Wes lowered him to the tunnel floor, where he sat down in the dust. He hated those words, *I can't.*

"One of you guys is going to have to do it," Jake said.

Wes looked up at the wall and then back to Amber. "I'm not the best climber, so maybe you should do it." He interlaced his fingers, and Amber stepped into his hands. She threaded her left foot into a gap in the rock. Then she reached her right hand toward a shallow stone shelf above her head. Jake watched as her fingers searched the narrow ledge.

"There's nothing up here." Her voice echoed through the tunnel. Wes lowered his hands, and she stepped back to the floor.

Struggling to his feet, Jake stared at the ledge and let out a long sigh.

"I hate to ask this," Amber began, "but could someone have got to the clue before us?"

Jake ignored her. He didn't want to even consider that someone else might have stumbled upon the clue or gotten to it before them.

Wes had walked toward the light of the tunnel exit and was now returning, holding his chin with two fingers, and tapping his lips.

"What are you thinking?" Jake asked.

"I think we paced it off from the wrong side." He pointed behind Jake to the tunnel entrance. "Maybe we were supposed to start from the exit, where the tunnel opens up to the bridge."

Amber scrambled toward the bridge side of the tunnel, set her heel against the metal of the bridge, and began marking her paces. "One, two, three..." Jake plodded to the location to watch.

"...Fourteen, fifteen." She stopped and faced the rock. Wes again supported her as she attempted to scale the wall.

"What are you guys looking for?" An unfamiliar voice called out.

Jake spun around, and Amber jumped down.

It was the older couple Wes had pointed out earlier. They walked toward the kids in the darkness, their bodies blocking the light from the tunnel entrance. A huge camera was slung over the man's shoulder, secured by a thick leather strap. As they got closer, the dim light revealed the friendly grins on their faces.

"Oh..." Wes began. "Nothing. We just thought this tunnel was...pretty cool and we're...doing some...some geology research."

"Geology research?" The man seemed surprised. "I thought school was out."

"Oh, it is. I just..." Wes fidgeted with the tube of his hydration pack. "I just really like...rocks."

The woman chuckled. "Well, young man, you've sure come to the right place. If you like rocks, you'll find plenty of them in the Grand Canyon."

The couple smiled as they walked past the kids and onto the bridge. Then the man turned around and said, "Have fun exploring."

"Will do," Wes called back.

As soon as they were out of earshot, Wes whispered, "I just don't trust those guys."

Amber shook her head. "You're being silly. I think they're nice."

"They're nosey."

"They were just being friendly," she replied. "Anyway, they're gone, so help me back up."

She leaned into the rock, her fingers exploring a series of small ledges and crevices. She accidentally knocked dust and dirt down onto her head. What didn't land in her hair sprinkled along the soft surface of the tunnel floor.

"There's a rock that's loose," she said. "Wes, can you push me up a bit?"

"I'm trying," he grunted.

"I can jiggle it, but it's jammed,"—she struggled—"Wes, I need to get higher."

"I'm giving it all I can," he groaned.

Jake mustered what strength he had left. He pushed away the pain pulsing through his knee and forehead. "I'll help." He placed his hands under Amber's other foot. She pressed hard and stretched toward the ceiling.

She leaned in and rested her shoulder against the wall. "Okay, I think I can get it now."

Jake's arms began to tremble.

"I need you guys to stay still."

"I'm trying," Jake snapped. He hated everything about this moment. He was too weak to climb. Amber was getting the clue. And now, his arms were giving out, but he didn't want to admit it.

"It's working," she said, her voice muffled because her lips were pressed so close to the rock wall. "Just...a...little... bit...more." She paused. "Got it!"

Jake's quivering arms gave out. Wes, still holding Amber's other foot, lurched forward into the dirt. Amber tumbled backward over Jake and landed awkwardly on the tunnel floor.

"Are you okay?" Jake breathed.

"I'm fine."

He could hear the frustration in her voice. She stood up, dusting herself off. "Next time, say something if you think you're going to drop me."

"Sorry," he mumbled.

"I know you're sorry," Amber replied. "I just need you to be honest with me in a situation like that." She held a square-shaped stone in her hand. "Here." She handed it to Jake. "It looks like someone chipped a space out of the wall and carved that rock so it would slide perfectly into the gap."

Jake turned the rock over. Amber was right; it wasn't just a random rock. Someone had definitely shaped it and smoothed its sides.

"I think there's something up there in the gap," Amber said. "I'll need another boost." Her eyes saw right through him, like she could read Jake's thoughts. "Can you do it?" she asked.

"Maybe for thirty seconds," Jake admitted. "That's all the strength I've got left."

"That's all we need," she replied.

She approached the rock, and both Jake and Wes knelt, offering their woven hands to support her again. Immediately, Jake's arms began shaking. He pressed his knee under his hands to keep them steady and prop them up.

"I feel something," she called out. "Guys, push me up a bit. I'm so close."

The boys pressed their legs and lifted.

"That's it. Perfect. I've got it."

They lowered Amber, and she hopped to the ground.

"Hold out your hand," she said to Jake.

He opened his palm, and she held a closed fist over his hand. She unfurled her fingers, and he felt the object hit his skin. It was small. But heavy. Amber pulled her fingers away to reveal the small, dark wooden tile that lay in Jake's trembling hand.

Wes hovered over it and gasped. "It's a perfect match," he whispered. "It looks just like the wood of the cube."

Jake smiled with satisfaction.

Then a voice boomed through the tunnel. "Excuse me." A tall man strode past them, nearly pushing them out of the way. When his shadowed body stepped from the dark tunnel into the light of the bridge, Jake saw the large yellow letters printed on the back of his blue jacket: FBI.

Jake turned around to see Wes's and Amber's stunned expressions. Then Wes whispered, "What in the world is the FBI doing here?"

CHAPTER 12

1880

Night crept over the world as the boys made their way back to the canyon rim. A yellow moon rose over the pine forests of the Kaibab Plateau, casting long sawtooth shadows of trees across their path. The narrow trail and rocky crags gave way to flat ground under the boughs of pinyon and ponderosa pines. Their citrus scent filled the night air as Nahmida led Abe through a world of dappled moonlight. When they emerged from the trees into a grassy clearing, Nahmida gestured for Abe to stop. He pointed at the ground near their feet, then knelt and began plucking beans from a thin, stringy stalk.

"My ancestors planted here in a time beyond memory," Nahmida explained. "The earth still bears good things." He walked carefully, trying not to crush any vines or stalks hidden among the knee-high grass. It was still early in the growing season, so the squash he found was small. Finding several, he added them to the beans, returned to Abe, and handed him half of the small meal. "We are lucky to have found these before the javelina did." Nahmida grinned, and Abe, though still in a weakened state, smiled back with gratitude.

"You'll need more than this; follow me." Nahmida plunged back into the woods. The boys ate as they walked through the dense forest until they came to a narrow wash, where the broad green leaves of currant bushes sprouted from the earth. The dark sheen of their berries glimmered in the silver light of the moon. Reaching a hand into the foliage, he plucked the cool, smooth berries and handed them to Abe.

"They are black and red currant berries," Nahmida explained.

Abe tossed them into his mouth.

"But, eat slowly, friend." Nahmida patted his stomach. "Or you'll get a bellyache."

Abe nodded, dark juice covering his teeth and lips.

They took off their shirts and filled them with what remained of the squash and beans before loading them with currants. Nahmida then led Abe down the wash and back to the rim of the great canyon. By now, the moon had risen high in the cloudless night sky.

"Without the clouds to hold the heat close to the ground, it will be cold tonight—too cold." Nahmida pointed along the rim to the east, where a faint, orange light flickered.

"It's them," Abe whispered. "We can't risk our own fire, can we?"

Nahmida shook his head. "No, but where we are going, it

will not be needed. And those men cannot afford to leave theirs. We will be safe."

They traveled to the edge of the canyon and, like bighorn sheep, scrambled down the side to a ledge where the sandstone was still warm. The rock radiated heat from the now-vanished sun.

"Plant your feet and lean out," Nahmida said.

"Lean out?" Abe asked, his voice uncertain.

Nahmida stretched out over the edge with him. Their faces were struck by a jet of warm air swooshing up the canyon wall. Their hair fluttered in its stream and warmed their skin.

"It is a special place where the heat of the canyon returns to the sky," Nahmida explained. "We'll be warm here."

The boys lay the remaining food on the ground, put on their shirts, and found the most comfortable spots to sleep. Surrounded by the rising drafts and cradled by the warm rock, their bodies relaxed. Nahmida stared at the stars and wondered how, in such a big world, he had crossed paths with this boy.

"Why are those men chasing you?" he asked.

Abe pulled a small wooden cube from his pocket and handed it to Nahmida. "Because of this."

Chapter 13

Phantom Ranch

Jake, Amber, and Wes stood in the tunnel and watched as the FBI agent crossed the suspension bridge.

"This is just weird." Amber brushed the dust and grit out of her hair with her hands. "An FBI agent at the bottom of the Grand Canyon. What do you think he's doing here?"

"I have no idea." Jake shrugged. "But you're right. It's weird." He flipped the wooden tile over and examined the carvings. "We need to fit this into the cube."

"You brought the cube?" Wes blinked rapidly and shook his head.

"It's in my pack," Jake replied. "But let's get to Phantom Ranch first. We're too out in the open here."

As they exited the cool air of

the tunnel and stepped onto the suspension bridge, a stifling wave of heat washed over them. It was immediately followed by a cool breeze rushing up from the river below. The bridge, longer than a football field, was one of only two spanning the Colorado River inside the Grand Canyon.

When they reached the middle of the bridge, they stopped for a moment and watched a blue river raft full of people pass underneath their feet. Wes waved down to them, but Jake was still feeling too nauseated to be friendly. He watched as they drifted by. A quiet anger simmered in his brain as he kept replaying the image of Amber grabbing the clue in the tunnel. It was *his* clue to find. Though he tried to shake the thoughts from his head, they kept coming.

"What do you think that tower thing is?" Amber pointed across the river to a slender stone tower built into the canyon wall. Rusted metal doors were spaced evenly along the structure.

"Whoa," Wes exclaimed. "How did you even see that thing? It blends right into the rock."

"We should keep moving," Jake mumbled and began trudging across the narrow bridge.

When they reached the other side, Wes stopped to read an interpretive sign, written to help tourists understand the place. "Check this out. The Black Bridge, also called the Kaibab Suspension Bridge, was built in 1929, and each of those cables"—he pointed to the long wire cords that suspended the bridge—"weigh a ton, like, literally a *ton* and were carried down here by men from the Havasupai tribe."

"Wait, it's over seven miles from the top of the canyon to the river. How's that even humanly possible?" Amber asked in disbelief.

"Yeah, and each cable was over five hundred feet long!" Wes added.

Jake had stopped at another sign. "Guys, there are ruins here, too."

Wes and Amber hurried to his side. Along the river were the remains of stone walls and a rock-lined pit. Several interpretive signs gave more details about the area, which was about the size of a small house.

Jake pointed to one of the words. "It says here these ruins are over a *thousand* years old. People called *Ancestral Puebloans* built this place and lived here."

"This is amazing," Amber replied.

Jake spun around slowly to take it all in: the bridge

arching across the river, the green water coursing through the canyon, and several rafts now beached on a stretch of brown sand. Behind him, the gray canyon walls rose into the sky, and just feet away were ancient ruins left by a people who lived in this very spot centuries ago. His moment of wonder was cut short by another surge of nausea. He sipped more water. But it didn't help.

The trail under their feet now followed the contours of the river. They were finally here, at the bottom of a canyon over a mile deep, in a place few people ever ventured to go. A chill went up Jake's spine. And though he still felt weak, exhausted, and sick, he knew in that moment he was exactly where he was supposed to be.

"This place keeps getting more amazing!" Wes gestured toward a verdant, tree-lined side canyon. "Phantom Ranch is back in there."

Following signs, they took a trail running alongside Bright Angel Creek, a small stream that began many miles away on the North Rim of the Grand Canyon. The trail led them into an oasis under the shade of cottonwood trees and blooming redbuds. They passed a small campground where other hikers had arrived and were setting up camp. As they traveled deeper into the canyon, its walls grew steeper and craggier. Hemmed in by its red and orange walls, Jake felt like he was stepping into a place kept secret from the rest of the world.

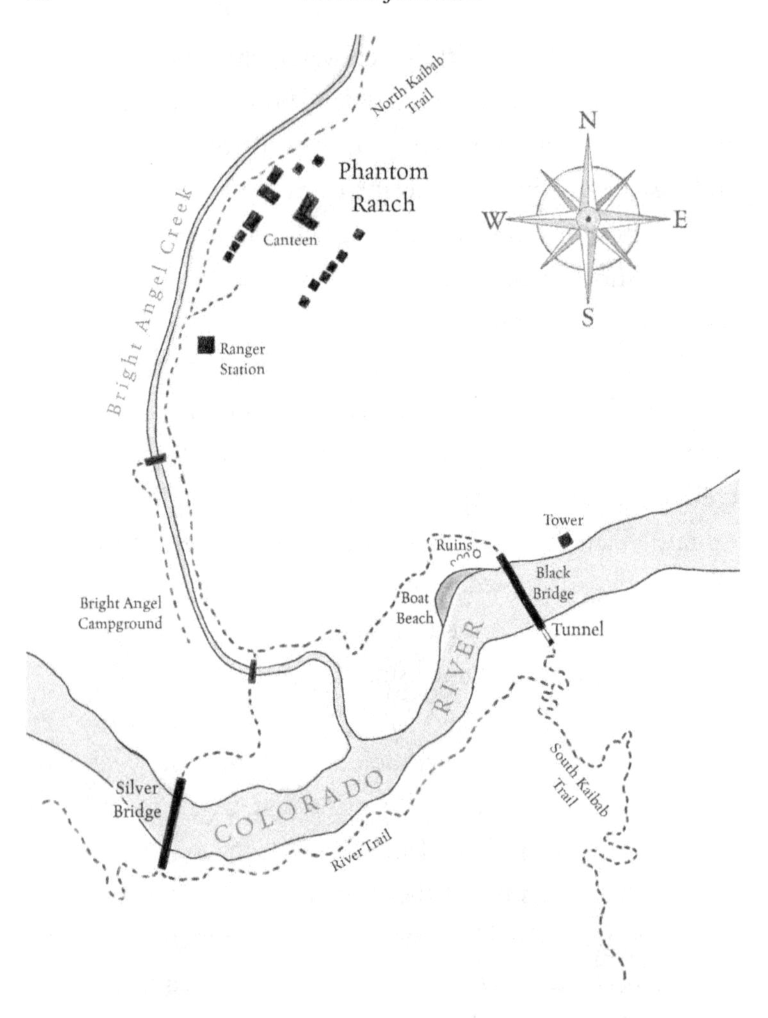

"What are these things?" Wes stopped beside a silver metal pipe with two arms. Glass insulators and copper wire hung at the end of each limb.

Trans-Canyon Telephone Line

"Looks like an old telegraph line. Or at least what's left of it," Jake said. "We've got them back in Ohio along the abandoned railroad tracks."

"Cool," Amber replied. "Hey, I think I hear our parents."

Amber and Wes took off down the trail, but Jake struggled along, not even attempting to keep up. *This bike turned out horrible.* He tried to push down the disappointment and resentment nagging his thoughts. His stomach roiled with nausea.

He saw his parents, and the tension in his body relaxed. They were outside the canteen, the largest building in

Phantom Ranch, a stone structure with green windows and dark-brown siding. The sign above them read: *Phantom Ranch Welcomes You.*

"You made it," Jake's mom said, giving him a squeeze. "Amber and Wes said you were having a hard time." She held him out by the shoulders and looked him over. "They also seemed really worried about you."

"I'm okay," he replied. "It might be heat exhaustion. That's what Wes read on a sign."

"Well, you certainly don't look okay." Her eyes lingered on his forehead. "What happened to your head?" She pulled off his ball cap and examined what had now become a yellow and blue bruise. "And your knee?"

Jake looked down at his blood-stained hiking pants. "It's

not that bad, Mom. I just slipped and fell."

"Hmmm." She tousled his hair and put his hat back on his head. Then she looked at Jake the way she did when she knew something was wrong. Her eyes turned serious. "Do you need to talk?"

He shook his head. "Not right now," he said quickly. "I'm okay."

"Well, Uncle Brian and Amber's dad have lunch going. How about you sit down and eat something? I'm going to have Aunt Judy take a look at you." His Aunt Judy was a nurse and would know what to do. His mom looked him in the eyes. "Jake, I'm here for you. Your dad is, too."

"I know," Jake said. "Thanks, Mom."

He settled down at a green picnic table in the shade of a massive cottonwood. His uncle was slicing meat and cheese. Jake looked around for Amber and Wes, but they had disappeared.

"You're probably wondering where they ran off to?" Mr. Catalina said. "They're checking out your cabins." He put some oranges and grapes on Jake's plate.

"Cool," he mumbled, trying to sound grateful for the information. *Thanks for ditching me, guys.*

Uncle Brian looked at Jake with concerned eyes. "Wes said you had a hard time on the way down."

"It wasn't that bad," Jake replied.

Just then, Aunt Judy arrived. "Sounds like I've got a patient."

Jake's mouth was full of food, so he nodded and forced a smile. She took his pulse. Aunt Judy was always calm. And she had a strength about her that somehow always made Jake feel stronger himself—even now when he felt so sick.

"And I heard you hit your head."

Jake took off his ball cap to reveal the bruise.

"How long ago?" she asked.

"About thirty minutes, maybe."

"Look at me." She stared into Jake's eyes. "Spell *world* backward."

"Why?"

"I'm trying to see if you have a concussion or not. That bruise on your head looks pretty serious."

"Okay, *D—L—R—O—W*."

"Good, now tell me what day of the week it is."

"Thursday."

"And the date."

"June sixth."

"Okay, now repeat these five words back to me: *alpha*, *bravo*, *charlie*, *delta*, *echo*."

Jake repeated them back to his aunt in the correct order. But as he did, his stomach muscles spasmed, and bile shot into his throat. He bent over and began throwing up onto the dusty ground.

Aunt Judy laid her hand gently on Jake's back as he continued to vomit.

When he finished, Jake sat back down at the picnic table, taking in a few deep breaths. His uncle found some dirt and covered up the mess he'd made on the ground.

"Did that help?" Aunt Judy asked.

"A little bit," Jake said. He was sweating, but the nausea

was gone.

She felt his forehead again. "Well, you've definitely got symptoms of heat exhaustion. It's not really bad—but it could get worse. So, I need you to do three things."

"First, put these in your water." She gave Jake a small purple packet. "They're electrolytes; they'll help your body recover. The next one is a bit unpleasant, but it's important. You need to take a very cold shower to bring your temperature down a few degrees. At least five minutes, okay?"

"Yeah, I promise," Jake answered.

"Then, get some rest. You might even take a nap. I'll check on you in about an hour."

"Yes, ma'am," Jake replied.

His aunt smiled. "I don't want anyone to miss tonight."

"What's going on tonight?" Jake asked.

"Campfire stories."

Wes dropped onto the bench beside Jake and grabbed a piece of cheese. "Mom, did you say, 'campfire stories'?"

"Sure did," his mom replied. "There's a wrangler who's been driving the mule train for thirty years, and he sometimes does a campfire night."

"Did you see the FBI agent?" Wes asked.

"We did. Kinda unusual, isn't it?" Uncle Brian replied as he unpacked some cookies and set them on the table. "I overheard him talking with the ranch manager. A girl went missing from here last week, and they can't find a trace of her anywhere."

Wes raised his eyebrows and looked at Jake. "Well, things just got weirder."

Chapter 14

1880

Nahmida turned the wooden cube over in his hand. He shook it, and something rattled inside.

"It's very old," he said. "Where did you find it?"

"Down in a cave in the Sangre de Cristo Mountains," Abe replied. "Nearly lost my life searching for it."

Nahmida studied the cube's markings in the moonlight. "Those men must believe it's valuable. Why did you bring it here?"

"I was told I could discover its meaning at the Grand Canyon," Abe replied.

Nahmida handed the cube back to him. "It's not from my people, but I know who can tell you where it comes from."

"Who are your people?" Abe asked.

"I am of the Havsuw' Baaj," Nahmida replied, "the people of the blue-green water. Our home is in the canyon, that way." He gestured to where the moon hovered high in the western sky.

"How did you learn to speak English?"

"From trading." Nahmida laced his fingers behind his head and leaned back against the rock. "I like to run," he explained. "Ever since I was small. And when I was big enough, I began trading with a Mormon settlement." He pointed to the east. "English is not so hard to learn. But it is more difficult than Spanish, Hopi, Paiute, and others."

"How many languages do you speak?"

Nahmida thought for a moment. "Six, well enough to trade." He closed his eyes. "We should sleep. I'll wake you early; we have a demanding journey tomorrow. I will take you to my people, and we will learn what this strange box of yours is trying to say."

Chapter 15

Campfire

"You boys are in cabin number two," Uncle Brian said. "It's back that way." He pointed with the knife he was using to cut up the meats and cheese.

"You feel well enough to go and get settled?" Wes asked.

"I've got to take a shower first. Doctor's orders." Jake handed the trekking poles back to Wes.

"You mean *my mom's orders.*" Wes gave his cousin a knowing look.

"The shower building is just south of your cabin," Uncle Brian explained. "While we are here, you kids are okay to explore, as long as you're staying between the bridges and the ranch. Outside that, I want an itinerary from you."

"Yes, sir," the boys said.

After his cold shower, Jake and Wes walked down the side-path to their cabin. It was nestled in the tall grass along the craggy walls of Bright Angel Canyon. Opening the green door, they were greeted by a rush of cool air.

"Air conditioning!" Wes stepped inside first. "I'm in heaven!"

Jake followed him into a small room with two sets of bunk beds. They each claimed a top bunk and threw their packs on the bottom ones.

"Check this out." Wes had opened a door into what looked like a small closet. "Our very own toilet room."

Jake laughed and looked inside to see a single toilet.

Just then, Amber appeared in the doorway. "Hey, guys, cool place, huh?"

Jake pretended not to hear her.

"Yeah, it's like we've stepped back in time," Wes replied. He climbed to the top bunk and began inspecting the exposed rafters. "It's the kind of place where your grandpa would have hidden clues."

Amber looked around the boys' cabin. "A famous architect, Mary Colter, designed most of these buildings—including this one."

Jake knew that he was supposed to rest, but the shower had worked, and he was already feeling a lot better. He pulled out the cube, unlocked it, and laid it flat on the mattress of the lower bunk. He placed the wooden tile Amber had found where his grandpa's drawing had indicated the location of missing piece #1. He turned it until the markings aligned. "It's a perfect fit."

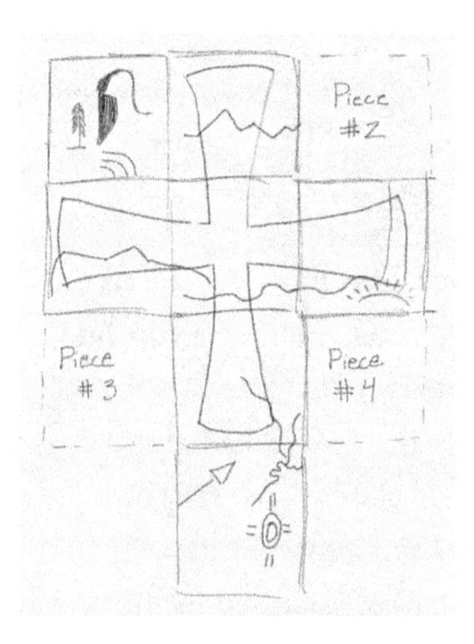

Wes climbed down from his bunk and dug through his backpack. Finding his sketch of the cube map, he sat down and began to draw in the first missing piece. "Here." Wes passed the paper to his cousin. "Now, what's our second clue?"

"*Gauging Station, Door 5.*"

"Could you tell us the other two," Amber asked, "just to remind us?"

Jake found her question irritating. *Why couldn't she just remember it?* "Number three says to *Find a Gate at Phantom Ranch*, and number four is *Granary at Indian Garden*."

"No, that's not it." Amber said.

"What do you mean, 'that's not it'?" Jake shot back. "I memorized these last night."

"Well, I don't remember it being *Find a Gate at Phantom Ranch*," Amber pushed back. "It was a single word, some kind of rock or mineral or something."

"Yeah," Wes chimed in. "I remember that, too."

Jake exhaled a long sigh through his nose and pulled his grandpa's letter from his back pocket.

"You're right," he said under his breath. "It's not a gate; *it's agate*."

"So, I wonder..." Amber began, tilting her head and biting her lip, "if your grandpa put the clues in the same order as our hike, then the gauging station would have to be somewhere between here and the tunnel."

"That doesn't make sense," Jake replied with frustration.

Amber furrowed her eyebrows. "Why are you being so crabby?"

"I'm not crabby," Jake snapped.

"Um." Wes's voice grew quiet. "That sounded pretty crabby."

Jake let out a huff. "Okay, say it again. I wasn't listening."

"Okay," Amber sighed. "I think the clues go in the order of our hike. Think about it: the first clue"—she tapped the wooden tile—"was in the tunnel, and the last one is at Havasupai Gardens."

"Wait, clue number four said something about a grain thing," Wes interjected, "at *Indian Garden*—not *Havasu...*whatever-you-said *Gardens.*"

"I know," Amber replied. "When Jake's grandpa wrote that clue, the place was called *Indian Garden*, but it was recently changed to honor the people who originally lived there, the Havasupai."

"How do you know all this stuff?" Wes asked.

"I read," Amber said in a playful tone. "There are a bunch of those interpretive signs around here, and they're really interesting."

Jake realized Amber was right, but he didn't want to admit it. Instead, he asked a question. "What if we look at the Grand Canyon map?"

"I'll go grab it from my things," Amber said. She left the boys and headed for her cabin.

"Jake, what's up with you?" Wes shrugged, lifting his hands. "You're being mean to Amber."

"I'm just kinda grumpy, I guess, from the heat and not feeling well."

"That's not a good reason to treat her like that. She's only trying to help."

Before Jake could respond, Amber opened the door and tossed Jake the map.

"Can I borrow your pencil?" Jake asked.

Wes handed it to him.

"Okay," Jake began, "if the clues are in order, then number one is here by the Black Bridge." He wrote a *#1* on the map by the location of the tunnel. "Number three, we know, is somewhere here at Phantom Ranch." He drew a *#3* near Phantom Ranch. "And the last clue is at Havasupai—" he paused. "This map still has it labeled as *Indian Garden*."

Amber and Wes leaned over to see while Jake wrote a *#4* beside the location.

"So, that would mean clue number two is somewhere between the tunnel and Phantom Ranch." Jake drew a light circle around the area between clue one and clue three. "It's somewhere in here." He tapped on the circle.

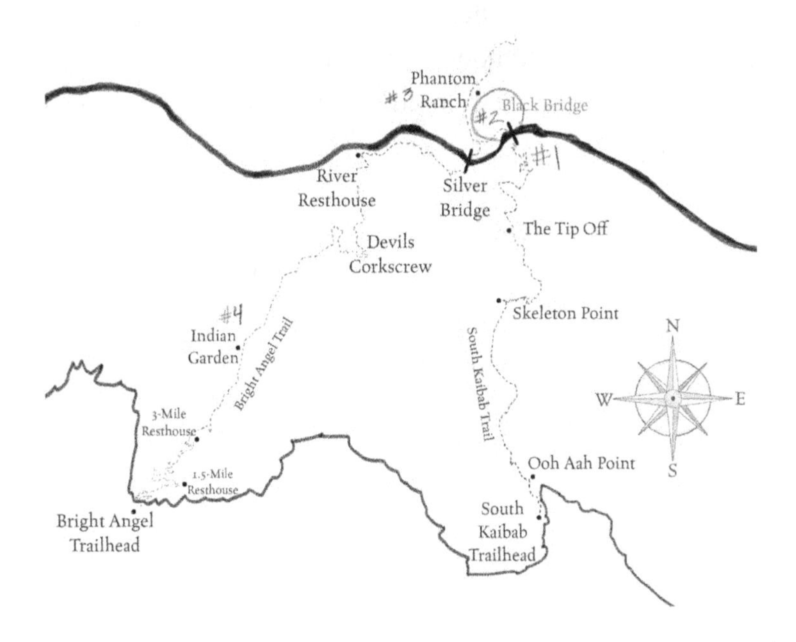

"That's exactly what Amber was saying," Wes said, looking Jake in the eyes.

"So, really, we're looking for *two* clues right now," she said.

Wes started pacing the small space between the bunks. "We're supposed to find agate. Okay, agate is a rock." He held one elbow with his right hand and tapped his chin with the other. Then he turned to Jake and Amber. "I've got good news and bad news," he said with a dramatic flair. "The bad news: there are rocks *everywhere*."

"And the good news?" Amber gave Wes an amused look.

"The good news is that an agate would stand out."

"What do they look like?" Jake asked.

"They're prettier than most of the rocks we've seen," Wes said. "Shinier, with different colors and swirls. People even make jewelry and stuff out of them. I'll keep my eyes peeled."

"If an agate is that special, then someone here would know about it," Amber offered. "I mean, it could be a rock used to build these cabins."

"Could be." Wes leaned back against the post of his bunk bed.

"The campfire guy," Jake said. "Your dad was saying that he's worked here for years. If anyone knows, it's him."

"And if the gauging station really is between here and the tunnel," Amber added. "He might know about that, too."

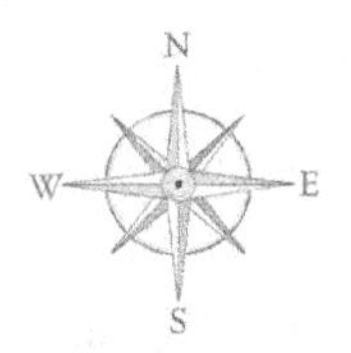

After a beef stew dinner in the canteen dining hall, the three families walked a darkening path to the campfire ring, where they sat down on log benches that encircled a crackling fire. Aunt Judy sat down beside him. "How are you feeling?"

"A lot better."

"Let me guess, you got dehydrated yesterday?"

"I did. I left my water bottle in the truck, and then just forgot."

"Well, lesson learned then." She nudged him with her elbow.

"Not exactly how I wanted to learn though." Jake sighed.

The older couple Wes had been so worried about earlier sat beside a man whom Jake assumed was the storyteller. His dirt-stained jeans showed proof of a hard day's work, and his calloused hands looked stronger than any Jake had ever seen. The wrangler's smile and laughter brought a lightheartedness to his sturdy and serious frame. After finishing his conversation with the couple, he leaned in toward the fire to warm his hands.

"Thanks, Ya'll, for coming tonight." He looked around at the families and hikers. "We cowboys have a tradition of telling stories over our fires at night. It helps us pass the lonely hours and make sense of things. From time to time, some of those stories take on a life of their own, and it becomes quite impossible to separate truth from fiction. The story I'm going to tell tonight is one of them kind."

The man had Jake's full attention.

"Just over a hundred years ago, there was a fella named Tom Watson. His friends gave him the nickname *Long Tom* on account he was so tall and lanky. Well, Long Tom was a rambler and couldn't stay put in Flagstaff for long before heading out with a pack mule into the Grand Canyon—in search of gold." The old rancher's eyes gleamed in the firelight.

"As he was wandering about, he stumbled upon an old, abandoned cabin and decided to settle in there for the winter. Of course, he needed some warmth, so he started rummaging through a bunch of old documents left in the place. He intended to use them to start a fire in the hearth. Just as he was about to set flame to the old papers, something caught his eye. In his hand"—the wrangler held up his fist—"he held an unopened letter."

Jake leaned in and wasn't surprised to see Wes and Amber doing the same thing.

"Well, he was curious, so he sliced the envelope open with his knife and began reading. The letter contained the last words of a dying man, a note intended for his brother. The hastily written script told how he had stumbled upon a large cache of gold nuggets in a canyon and gathered them up in a leather sack. On his way out, he was attacked by bandits. Well, it's one thing to get yourself beat up by a bunch of fellers in the middle of nowhere. But it's another thing to have your gold stolen. So what do you think he did?" The cowboy waited a second or two for dramatic effect. Jake tried to imagine the man's options. "He tossed that sack through the shimmering curtain of a waterfall, where it landed on a ledge of rock.

"Long Tom flipped the letter over and found a map scribbled onto the back, noting the location of the waterfall. Just as soon as he could, he loaded up a mule and started his search for the treasure. The map wasn't so good, and he spent nearly a year scouring canyon upon canyon for the gold. First, he searched out the big waterfalls—and there's a bunch here in the Grand Canyon and its side canyons. But there's also a lot of intermittent ones, waterfalls that only run after a hard rain. So, he starts looking for waterfalls that ain't waterfalls at all, looking for spots where the water once coursed and washed the cliffside clean or left a white streak of mineral deposits.

"Well, one day, he finds a seasonal waterfall, one that matches the map and the description in the dead man's letter. Problem is he has to climb up to reach it. So, Long Tom scrambles up and climbs further, until he finds a ledge, and behind the ledge, there's a nook. And in that nook, he sees the rotten leather of a saddlebag and the cache of gold nuggets layin' there in a pile around it. Well, let me tell you, when he saw the gold, his whole body got to buzzin' with excitement.

"While Long Tom had been climbing and taken with the sight of the treasure, a big storm had come up. Dark clouds covered the sun, and rain began trickling down on the crumbling sandstone. Tom decided to fetch something to carry the nuggets down in—'cause there was a lot of 'em. However, on his way down, Tom slipped on some rain-slicked rock and took a mean tumble. He slid down the canyon wall and busted up his leg real bad.

"Tom left the treasure behind and somehow got himself onto that mule and out of the canyon. After he recovered, he went back to reclaim the treasure, but he never did locate the spot. So, somewhere out here"—he pointed into the darkness, and his hand glowed in the firelight—"there's a treasure of gold nuggets just laying on a ledge of rock waitin' for someone to discover it."

Wes, who looked completely enthralled with the man's story, leaned forward and asked, "What happened to the letter and map?"

"No one knows for sure," the storyteller answered.

Jake gazed over the top of the cottonwood trees behind the wrangler to where the light of the half-moon lit the sawtooth ridge of the canyon that hemmed in Phantom Ranch. The leaves of the tallest trees quaked in a cold breeze that surged through the valley. For a few moments, everyone remained silent, caught in the sense of wonder brought by the words of the story and the night wind.

In the distance, Jake noticed the faint beam of a flashlight cutting through the darkness behind the canteen building. It vanished just as quickly as it had appeared. But then a shadow moved, and Jake could swear that it scaled the side of the building. *What the heck?* His eyes darted to Wes and Amber, but like everyone else, they had been staring into the dancing flames of the campfire.

The older couple thanked the storyteller and headed back to their cabin for the night. Wes watched them with narrowed eyes. Jake elbowed him. "Wes, stop it. They're not up to anything."

"Didn't you see earlier?" Wes replied. "Before they came to the fire? They were at the FBI agent's cabin—and for a long time."

That was odd, Jake thought. "There probably is a good reason, Wes. Anyway, we should ask him." Jake gestured toward the old wrangler.

Jake, Amber, and Wes scooted over on the log bench to get closer to the cowboy.

"Thanks for the story," Jake began. "We were wondering if we could ask you a couple of questions?"

"Sure thing, but if it's about the treasure, I've told ya all I know."

"Actually, we were wondering if you knew anything about a gauging station?" Jake asked.

The man let out a laugh, leaned his elbows on his legs, and clasped his hands. "Well, that's a question I've never been asked."

In the pause, Jake was afraid the cowboy didn't know. And if *he*—a man who had lived and worked down here for decades—didn't know, then who else possibly could?

But to Jake's relief, the cowboy had something to say on the subject. "Well, a lot of folks miss it—don't even know it exists—'cause it's built out of the same rock as the canyon walls. If you're hiking from here, it's just upstream from the bridge. Looks like a big chimney."

"We saw that stone tower thing when we were walking across the bridge," Wes said. "Is that it?"

"Yes, that's the gauging station."

The three kids looked at each other, eyes wide in the soft, orange light.

"Before they built the Glen Canyon Dam," the man continued, "back in the 1960s, the water in the Colorado River would flow up the sides of that tower, and they could take measurements. Now, they use high-tech stuff. There's gear in the tower, and you'll notice a solar panel up on top. It's likely a remote site now, beaming the river flow information to a satellite or something."

"Thank you," Wes said. "If it's okay, we've got one more question for you. And it's probably another that nobody's ever asked you."

"Shoot," the man said.

"We're wondering if there are any agate rocks here at Phantom Ranch?"

The old man wrinkled his brow and cocked his head to the side. "I couldn't say. I've seen agates before, but not here in the canyon. I've stumbled upon some fossils, like trilobites and brachiopods, but not any agates." He paused to think for a moment. "I guess you could ask the ranger tomorrow or the manager here at Phantom Ranch."

"Thanks, sir," Jake said.

The wrangler got to his feet and said goodnight to everyone. Then he took a moonlit path into the night.

"Dad, Mom," Jake said. "Can we go back to the cabin and make our plans for tomorrow?"

"As long as your plans don't include scaling canyon walls looking for that lost treasure," his dad said.

Jake could feel his face get red. "Dad, we're not going to do something that stupid."

His dad gave him an I-don't-know-if-I-believe-you look. "I know you're feeling better, but you're going to need some good sleep tonight. Lights out at ten o'clock, okay."

"Will do," Jake replied.

The cabin's stone exterior was illumined by the quivering light of the campfire. The three kids hurried down the path, burst inside, and flopped down on the bunks.

"Okay," Wes asked, "What's our plan?"

"We go to the gauging station first thing in the morning," Jake replied.

"And we ask about the agate," Amber added.

"Definitely." Jake paused for a moment, replaying in his mind the shadow behind the canteen building. "Hey, did you guys see that light behind the canteen tonight during the campfire?"

Wes and Amber shook their heads.

"Somebody was back there with a headlamp or a flashlight."

"It was probably just one of the people who work in the kitchen," Wes said. "There's trash cans back there. I bet someone was just taking out the garbage."

"But it gets a little weird," Jake added, leaning his forearms across his legs. "After the light went out, I could swear I saw someone climb up the side of the building."

"That's really strange," Amber said.

"You sure it wasn't an animal?" Wes offered. "Maybe one of those big squirrels like we saw at the sand dunes?"

"No, it was big. Like *human* big."

"Maybe it was a sasquatch." Wes grinned.

Jake gave his cousin a push, and Wes fell backward on the bed. "I'm *serious*. I saw something."

Amber looked at her watch and stood. "It's almost ten. We should get to bed."

"Wait," Wes said, getting up and standing between the bunks. "Before Amber leaves, we should do our hand stack."

The three friends stacked their fists, counted to three, and dropped their hands.

Chapter 16

The Gauging Station

When Jake woke, Wes was still asleep in the other bunk bed. He ambled outside, where he found Amber at the picnic table, drawing in her journal. Wanting to avoid her, he turned back toward the cabin.

"Good morning," he heard her say as he placed his hand on the door handle. His plan to slip away silently had failed.

"How are you feeling?" she quietly called to him.

"Way better," he answered. He walked over and sat down across from her. "That's pretty good," he remarked. "I didn't know you were an artist."

She smiled and set her pencil down. "I just like drawing." She paused. "Jake, I feel like you're upset with me. Was there something that I said or did yesterday?"

Jake shook his head. "No, just the heat exhaustion stuff. I'm sorry for being so grumpy." The apology didn't feel true in his heart, and Amber noticed.

"Are you sure?"

"No," Jake said quickly. "I mean, yes. I'm sure." It was too threatening to think about what he really felt, that he was tired of her being better at *everything*. It felt like an impossible jumble inside of him, and he had no idea how to put it into words. Instead of trying, he said, "We're good."

"Okay," Amber said, but she sounded unconvinced. She went back to drawing.

The last thing he wanted to say was, "I'm tired of *you* being better at *everything*. And I wish you hadn't found the clue yesterday. It was meant for *me*—not you." Thinking this was one thing. But to say it felt childish.

The cabin door slammed shut, and Jake spun around to see Wes wandering toward them, looking as if he had just wrestled a wild animal. His shirt was crumpled, and his hair was sticking up everywhere like a mad scientist on a camping trip. He plopped down beside Jake and let out a low grunt.

"Good morning, Wes," Amber said in a quiet and friendly voice.

"Morning," Wes mumbled, rubbing the sleep out of his eyes. "What time is it?"

Amber checked her watch. "Six fifty-five."

"That means they're serving eggs and bacon at the canteen in five minutes," Jake said.

At the word *bacon*, Wes immediately woke from his stupor.

"Did you just say *the magic word*?"

"I sure did."

Wes sprang from his seat and ran back to the cabin to change.

Amber laughed, and it made Jake feel better.

"Jake, I don't know what's going on. But when you figure it out, I'd like to talk about it."

Jake nodded. "Sure. Okay." But inside, he was hoping she'd forget and it would all just go away.

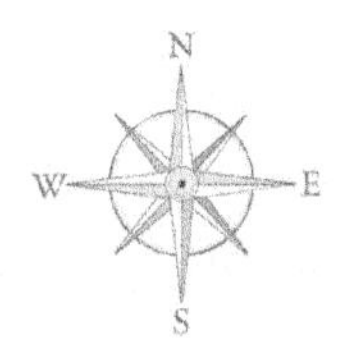

After breakfast, the kids gave Uncle Brian their itinerary and promised to return by lunch. They sprinted down to the river and began following the trail upstream. Past the Black Bridge, the path narrowed, and Jake took the lead. When they reached a rock outcrop above the gauging station tower, they located a faint series of tight switchbacks. At the end of the path, they scrambled down a short rock face and dropped onto a strip of wet sand along the river. The tower, like a pillar of stone, rose from the sand into the sky.

"Dang!" Wes looked up at the top of the tower. "This thing is wicked cool."

"And see the doors?" Amber pointed up. "It's just like the clue said. There are *five* of them."

Jake stared up at the metal doors. The first was rectangular and stood at ground level. He reached out and pulled on it, but the hinges were seized with rust. Wes and

Amber gripped the corroded metal, and Jake counted, "One, two, three, pull!"

The kids wrenched the door open a few inches as the hinges creaked like nails on a chalkboard.

They covered their ears as the screeching reverberated along the sandstone walls of the canyon.

"Oh my gosh," Wes said. "That was the worst thing ever."

"Well, we've got to do it again." Jake winced. "Or we're not getting inside."

Tentatively, they all grabbed the door a second time, and on Jake's count, they yanked as hard as they could, prying the door just wide enough for Jake to slip inside.

"It might be easier if I push on the door from in here," Jake said. "I can hold it open so you guys can get in."

Amber and then Wes squeezed through the narrow gap between the door and the stone wall. The dark, musty room was confining and creepy. Wes backed into the stone wall, setting a huddle of pill bugs scattering across his arm.

"Ahhh," he yelled and jumped, bumping into Amber. "What is that? Get it off me!"

Amber brushed the pill bugs off his sleeve. "It's just a few rollie pollies," she said, her voice a calm contrast to his panic.

A metal ladder bolted to the stone wall led up to a rickety-looking wooden platform. Jake went first, followed by Amber, and then Wes.

"I don't trust this old floor to hold all three of us," Wes said. "I'm going to wait down at the bottom while you guys go find the clue." He cautiously stepped back onto the ladder and climbed down.

Amber and Jake looked up into the darkness. "I wish we'd thought to bring a headlamp," Amber murmured. "At least I brought my phone." She switched on the flashlight and handed it to Jake. "Could you shine it up there while I go?"

Why does she always have to go first? Jake wondered. *She probably wants to be the first person to find the clue.* He looked up at the rusted ladder and the rotten wood.

"I can go second," Amber offered, "if you'd rather go first."

"No, it's fine," Jake lied. "I'll take your phone." He held out his hand. His response felt dishonest—because it was. But part of him wanted Amber to go first so he could hold onto the story he'd made up in his head.

Amber grabbed the rungs of the ladder and hoisted herself up to the third floor. "It's kinda gross up here," she called down. "Bird poop all over the place."

Jake followed, and handed the phone up to Amber. He needed both hands to safely ascend the ladder. She shined the light on door three. "Just two more, and we're there." She gave the phone back to Jake.

He took a step backward, and a floorboard creaked underfoot. Something slender and cold touched his back. Spinning around, he encountered a tarnished metal cable running through a small hole in the ceiling above him and through a similar opening in the floor at his feet. "Wonder what that's for?" He cast the flashlight's beam to the ceiling. "It must be connected to something up at the top."

"Well, let's find out." Amber pulled herself up to the fourth floor. Jake followed. The metal ladder ended here, but someone had propped an aluminum step ladder against the wall.

"There's at least one more level to go," Amber said, staring up at the dark opening in the ceiling.

She and Jake unfolded the step ladder. Here, the ceiling was higher, and the ladder was barely tall enough for them to reach the top. "We're going to have to use that step on top that says, 'Not a step'." Amber grinned as she stepped onto the blue plastic top of the ladder. As she did, it wobbled, and Jake threw his hand out to steady it. "Thanks," she said, breathing a sigh of relief. "I'm going to have to jump to make it up there. You've got the ladder, right?"

"I've got it," Jake replied. "You can do it." Jake felt his frustration with Amber fading. He didn't know exactly why, and now wasn't the time to figure it out.

Amber jumped into the opening. Supporting herself first with her hands, she lunged forward onto her belly, and then army-crawled across the floor. Jake watched, memorizing her moves so that he could do the same. "Your turn," her voice called from the darkness.

Jake climbed the ladder and handed her the phone. After finding a place for it, she reached out for one of Jake's hands. "I'll pull when you jump. Just tell me when."

Jake nodded and gingerly stepped onto the not-a-step step. "Okay, on the count of three."

"Wait," Amber said. "Are you going to jump on three? Or are you going to count and then jump? I don't want to yank your arm off."

Jake smiled. "Let's go on *jump.*"

"Okay, ready when you are," she said.

"One, two, three, jump!" Jake sprang up as Amber pulled. He landed on his knees, sending gray dust into the air.

The cable Jake had discovered on the floor below terminated at an old, green metal box covered with dials and switches. "This thing is cool," Jake remarked. "I bet it's what they used to measure the water flows back in the day."

"Jake, shine the light over here." She tugged at a frayed burlap sack lying on the floor. Pulling it aside, she uncovered a backpack. It looked almost new and packed with all kinds of gear. All sorts of rock climbing equipment had been attached to its sides with carabiners. Amber unsnapped the clasps that secured the top compartment. Inside, she found a red dry bag stuffed with dehydrated food.

"This is a weird place to stash a pack like that," Jake said.

"Yeah, strange," Amber said as she buckled the pack and covered it with the burlap.

As she did, Jake approached the southern wall and found the square casement of the metal door. "Door number five," he breathed to himself. He pressed on the metal. Like the one at the entrance, it was frozen shut. A thin slice of light shone around its edges. Casting the phone's light on the doorsill, he could see nothing but rock, dust, and more bird droppings.

Amber sidled up beside him. "Maybe it's hidden behind

another loose stone," she offered. "Like the clue in the tunnel."

They began tugging on the rocks along the casement, but they were all securely cemented in place.

"Wait!" Amber said. "Jake, shine the light on the door—the metal part."

The light revealed a faint square etched into its bronze and rusty surface. Within the square, Jake recognized markings similar to the ones on the cube and the wooden tile they'd found in the tunnel.

"This is it!" Jake gave Amber a high five. "We found it."

"But it's not a tile." Amber replied.

"You're right. But look at the markings; it's definitely the clue."

"We need to think bigger then," Amber mused. "Clues

three and four could be wooden tiles, or they could be something more like this."

Jake studied the etching in the door.

"Well, what are you waiting for?" Amber asked. "Take a picture."

He opened the photo app and snapped a shot of the door. The room was so dark the flash was temporarily blinding. He flipped the camera around to see the perfect image of the clue.

"We'll ask Wes to draw it into the map," Amber said.

The two kids lowered themselves down the precarious aluminum ladder and then stored it against the wall where they found it. They descended the rungs of the old metal ladder until their feet landed on the soft earth of the ground floor.

Wes stood, his face pressed against the entrance, peering out the gap in the door.

"What are you doing?" Amber asked.

"That old couple," Wes said. "They followed us."

"What do you mean?" Jake asked.

"I mean, they're standing on the bridge, and the guy has that big camera pointed right at us."

Chapter 17

1880

Nahmida and Abe finished what remained of the currant berries as the first light of the sun crowned the eastern horizon. The fire they had seen the night before was snuffed out. Either the men were still asleep, or they were lurking somewhere in the forest. Either way, Nahmida knew the men would be weakened by their hunger and thirst and from a long night trying to keep warm.

"I should have asked you this earlier." Nahmida looked earnestly into Abe's eyes. "Can you swim?"

"I can," Abe replied. "I'm not the best, but good enough."

Nahmida certainly hoped so. He led Abe down a series of meandering paths that twisted along the canyon walls. As the sun rose and the heat intensified, they came to a deep and narrow ravine that looked impassible. "The ancient-ones built bridges," Nahmida explained. "We still use them. But be careful; they are very old." Before them stood a primitive structure built of pine logs and woven with branches. To an untrained eye, it would have gone unnoticed.

The boys bear-walked across on their hands and feet. Halfway, Nahmida looked down to see the stream cutting through the ravine two hundred feet below. Though he had crossed this way countless times, his stomach still lurched. A fall here would be deadly. The creek was a sliver of white against the red stone of the canyon, but its distant rumble rose to their ears.

They traveled hidden trails for hours. Nahmida showed Abe ancient granaries built high into the sides of the sandstone cliffs. "The ancient-ones built them to house their food, far from mice." They quenched their thirst and cooled their feet at a hidden waterfall that shot like a spout from the canyon wall.

Later in the day, Nahmida knelt on the ground and began pulling away a stack of rocks. "Friend, come here." He beckoned to Abe. "You'll like this." Nahmida uncovered a cached pottery vessel buried in the earth. "When I travel, I leave food here." He reached in and drew out a small chunk of honeycomb and handed it to Abe. "The ground keeps it cool, and the pot keeps the bugs out." He examined his piece and smiled. "Well, most of the time."

In the afternoon, their path began to descend toward the river. Nahmida pointed out a broad bend where the water appeared still. "That is where we will cross."

"But the river is so wide there," Abe replied.

"Yes, you're right," Nahmida answered. "But the water is much stronger in the narrow places and difficult to cross."

Their path snaked along cramped ledges and over crumbling rocks as it wound its way down to the river. Nahmida's heart was cheered by the murmur of the water and a cool breeze that coursed along the canyon walls. But there was another sound. He halted and cocked his ear toward the rim.

"What is it?" Abe whispered.

"They've followed us."

Upstream and above them, a slide of gravel and sand set loose. The cascading rocks hit a ledge and shot into the air. A trickle of falling silt and stones was followed by silence.

Then, a gunshot rang out above the din of the river.

The boys sprinted across a series of rocky shelves that, like stairs, ran down to a small orange-colored, sandy beach. Nahmida flattened himself against a low wall and pulled Abe back with him.

"Upstream. Over there." Nahmida pointed to where two haggard-looking men, rifles at their sides, were struggling down the narrow path.

"We can't cross. And we can't stay," Nahmida said. "We'll have to jump—and let the river take us."

Chapter 18

Bugging Out

Jake peeked out the door. Wes was right: the couple stood on Black Bridge, and the man, pointing his camera at the gauging station, appeared to be taking pictures with his telephoto lens.

"I have a theory," Wes whispered. "You know how the looters at the sand dunes were working for the bad guys?"

Amber and Jake nodded.

"Well, what if the couple is working for them, too?" Wes scratched his head. "It's the perfect disguise."

"It is a little weird for them to be just standing up there taking photos," Amber remarked. Jake agreed.

"We can't let them see us," Wes said, peeking out the slit in the doorway. "And we can't stay in here."

"We can always wait," Amber replied. "Maybe they'll leave."

"On the third floor..." Jake began, "I think there was another door. One that didn't face the river. Maybe we could escape that way. It's so rocky up there. They probably wouldn't see us."

"It's worth trying," Amber said, turning on her phone's flashlight again and handing it to Jake.

Wes let out a deep sigh. "Okay, but I was hoping I wouldn't have to go up there."

"What are you afraid of?" Jake asked.

"What wouldn't I be afraid of?" Wes answered. "Heights, for one. Hantavirus. Histoplasmosis."

"Histo-what?" Jake asked.

"Histoplasmosis. It's a disease you can get from bird and bat poop."

Jake snickered. "Wes, we're going to be up there for, like, two minutes. You'll be fine." He handed the phone up to Amber, who had already climbed the ladder. Wes followed.

On the third level, the phone's flashlight revealed another short doorway hidden behind a curtain of cobwebs. Jake brushed them away to find another thick and rectangular metal door.

"This one still has a handle," Jake said, giving it a tug. "I bet it's been shut for, like, fifty years."

The three kids pulled on the door with all of their strength until the frozen hinges made a popping sound, followed by a long, whining creak. A thin shaft of light cast across the floor, and illuminated specks of dust floated in the air.

"Amber, you take the handle," Jake said. "Wes, grab the bottom of the door. I'll grab the top."

"But there's a ton of mouse poop down here."

"Okay, I'll take the bottom part," Jake replied. "You take the top."

As they pulled, the door screeched and groaned, opening just enough for a way out. After squeezing through the opening, they pulled the door closed and scrambled up the crag to regain the trail.

The older couple was nowhere to be seen. Not on the bridge. Not on the path.

"It's like they disappeared," Wes said, wiping sweat from his brow. "Ughh, it's already getting hot again."

As they turned onto the trail for Phantom Ranch, they noticed a large corral that was empty yesterday. Now it was teeming with mules. One of the mule wranglers leaned against the corral fence, talking with the FBI agent. Jotting down notes on a small notepad, the agent appeared to be asking the young man a series of questions. The kids slowed their pace in an attempt to eavesdrop.

"When was the last time you saw her?" the agent asked.

"I guess about two weeks back," the wrangler replied. "She'd come from Phantom Ranch to help us brush out the mules. Awful pretty girl."

"Did she say anything about an artifact?"

"What do you mean?" the wrangler asked.

"Did she mention finding something here in the canyon, perhaps something of historical significance?"

The wrangler shook his head. "No, she never mentioned anything like that. She was more into animals and rock climbin'."

The kids kept walking, trying not to draw attention to themselves.

"I wonder if that girl stole something?" Wes asked, walking backward and facing the other two. "Maybe it's like at the sand dunes, and we've got another looter to catch." He smiled and rubbed his hands together.

Along their path, a piece of paper had been stapled at eye-level to the trunk of a cottonwood tree. Though it was still far off, Jake could make out the big black letters: MISSING. He ran to the tree. A black and white photocopy featured the face of a young woman; she looked to be about his brother Nick's age. She had a broad, energetic smile. Her hair was pulled back and tucked under a ball cap with embroidered letters that read *NOLS*. Below the photo was printed: *Agatha Albright: Age 18, 5' 4", 110 lbs, brown eyes, brown hair.*

"This would be a terrible place to go missing," Amber said.

"Yeah," Wes agreed. "Remember at Rocky Mountain National when my dad was telling us about the ways people die in the wilderness? This place has all three." He began counting them off on his fingers. "It would be easy to drown here, to fall, or even freeze to death at night. And as a nice bonus, there's the heat." He wiped his brow with the bottom of his T-shirt. "All kinds of ways to become worm food."

"That's kinda gloomy, Wes," Amber replied. "She could be alive."

"I'm just being realistic."

"Come on, guys," Jake beckoned. "Let's get back and fit this clue into the map."

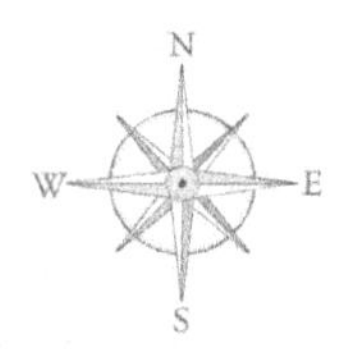

Back in the cabin, the boys sat on their bunks and Amber pulled up a chair. Wes studied the photo of the clue and began sketching it onto the cross-shaped map. "It matches up perfectly." He lifted the paper and showed it to Jake and Amber.

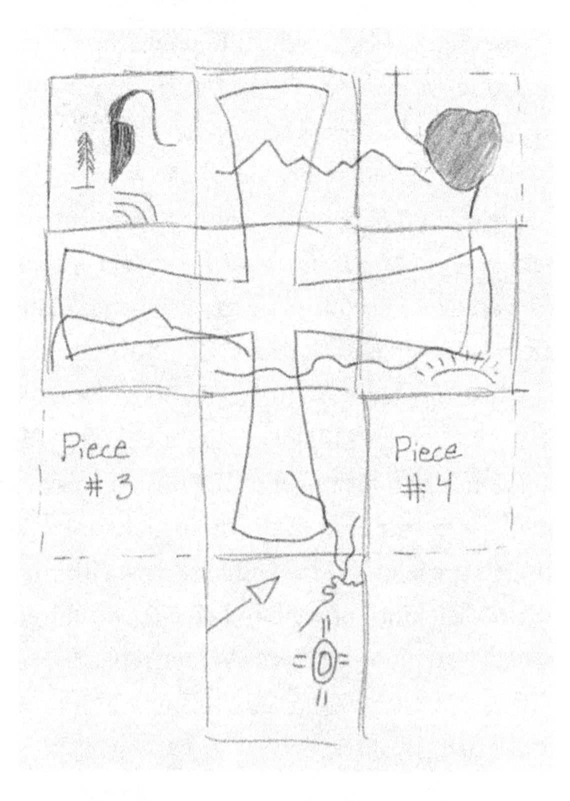

"Nice work," Jake said, impressed with his cousin's drawing. "We've got the gauging station clue and the tunnel clue. Now we just need to find the agate."

"When do we leave Phantom Ranch?" Wes asked.

"The day after tomorrow," Jake replied. "So, we have two days."

Amber got up from the chair. "What if you guys go talk to the ranger while I find the ranch manager?"

"Good plan," Jake replied. "Let's go."

The boys found the ranger at the Phantom Ranger Station. Hearing their question, she squinted her eyes. After a moment, she raised a finger, like she had remembered something. Then she walked into the back room. Jake could hear other voices. She returned with a folded brochure in her hand. "Sorry, boys, no agates here that we know of. But if you two are rockhounds, this might interest you." Jake took the paper that read, *Journey Through Time: Grand Canyon Geology*. Wes took it from Jake and immediately began reading.

Disappointed, they returned to the cabin, where Wes finished reading the brochure and began dealing out cards. "You ever play Golf?"

"You can play golf with cards?"

"Yeah, I'll teach you."

The boys were into the second round of their card game when Amber burst through the door.

"You won't believe what I found out."

"What?" Jake asked.

"Can you get that letter from your grandpa out?"

"Sure." Jake dug through his backpack, found it, and handed the paper to her.

She unfolded it, glanced down, and her mouth dropped open.

"What?" Jake asked. "What is it?"

She slowly handed the letter back to him. "Look at the clue, Jake."

Jake studied the words: *Find Agate at Phantom Ranch*. "I don't see anything," Jake replied.

"The letter *A*—it's capitalized," Amber said. "Agate is not a *rock*. It's a *person*."

"A person?" Wes stood up from his mattress, sending his well-organized cards into a jumble.

"It's her nickname. Agatha Albright's nickname."

"Wait," Jake said. His eyes shot open, and his mouth followed. "You mean the girl from the missing person poster?"

Amber smiled, slowly nodding her head. "The ranch manager said Agate started working at the canteen this spring. One day last week, she just didn't show up for work. Her best guess was that she went for a solo hike and got lost."

"So, we were supposed to come to Phantom Ranch to find a girl," Wes said, holding his palm to his forehead. "But now she's gone missing, or..." Wes's face became grave. "I hate to say this—she might be dead."

"How long has she been gone?" Jake asked.

"The ranch manager said that this is day eight." Amber's face fell. "So, that's not good."

"Not good at all." Wes looked at the ground.

Amber rubbed her chin with her thumb and forefinger. She closed her eyes and appeared deep in thought. Her eyes flashed open. "Jake, the backpack."

"What backpack?"

"The one at the top of the gauging station."

"Wait. You guys found a bag in there?" Wes asked.

"Yeah," Amber replied. "It had climbing gear, survival food, clothes, and stuff. I remember looking at the climbing shoes and thinking they would fit me. She is almost my same height and weight."

"How do you know that?" Jake asked.

Wes shot his finger out at Amber. "From the poster! It said she was five foot..."

"Five foot four inches," Amber replied. "I'm five foot three inches."

"From how you described it, it sounds like a bug-out bag," Wes said.

"A what?" Amber's eyes crinkled.

"A bug-out bag. It's a survival bag that you pack with all the stuff you need in case of an emergency," Wes explained. "Like how we always pack the Ten Essentials when we hike, right?"

Jake and Amber nodded.

"A bug-out bag has all that but *more*," Wes added. "It's going to have food and other gear you need to survive for several days while you get to safety or wait to be rescued."

"So, wait," Jake said, almost bursting out of his seat. "If it's Agate's bag, then it means she was planning to run, to escape."

"From what?" Wes asked.

"Your guess is as good as mine," Jake replied. His body buzzed with the sense that something invisible and dangerous was at play.

"And if she didn't run," Amber began, "then she's either lost or..."

"Or she's dead," Wes replied.

Amber slapped his shoulder with the back of her hand. "Quit saying stuff like that."

"I'm just saying." Wes rubbed his shoulder. "This is a bad place to be lost."

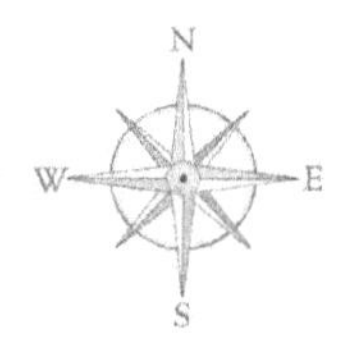

That night the families gathered for dinner in the Phantom Ranch dining room again. Plates and all the fixings to build your own burritos sat on long tables. The paned windows reminded Jake of the flattened cube and its tiles. Wes had befriended the kitchen staff and was chatting them up about dessert.

Jake was studying the ceiling when Wes returned. Pulling a chair out, he announced, "Chocolate cake!" He followed Jake's gaze, scrunching his face up, trying to discern what Jake found so interesting.

"What in the world are you looking at?"

"The ceiling," Jake replied. "It's big."

Amber entered late and sat beside Jake. She followed

Jake's and Wes's eyes to look at the ceiling. "What's going on?"

"Jake here is pondering the size of the ceiling," Wes replied. "Which reminds me: I have a great joke about ceilings."

Jake stopped and looked at his cousin. "What's the joke?"

"I'd try to explain it," Wes replied. "But it would just go over your head."

Amber let out a long sigh. "*Wes*, that's so terrible."

Jake just shook his head. "I was checking out the ceiling because—"

"Wait," Wes interrupted, "I know why."

Jake leaned forward on his elbows. "Okay, then tell me."

"Because," he drew out the word, "you think it's the best ceiling in the world."

Jake snickered, "No, that's not why. I was—"

"I mean, it's not the *best*," Wes interrupted again, "but *it's up there*." Wes pointed to the ceiling and grinned at his own joke.

Jake sighed and palmed his forehead. "I can't believe I walked right into that."

Amber groaned. "Please, no more ceiling jokes." She looked at Jake and raised her eyebrows. "I want to hear what Jake was doing."

"I was thinking," Jake began, "that there's got to be a room above the dining hall. But I can't see a way to get up there. No stairs, no ladder, nothing."

Amber and Wes began surveying the room.

"But here's the thing: *there's a window up there*. I saw it from outside." Jake pointed to the ceiling with his thumb. "So, there's got to be some kind of room. An attic or something."

Wes continued staring at the ceiling.

"Hey, Wes," Amber said, tapping the table. "You must have a lot of respect for that ceiling."

He looked at her in confusion. "What do you mean?"

"You really look up to it." She smirked.

"And you think my jokes are terrible." Wes gave her a disapproving look. "And *after* you stipulated, 'no more ceiling jokes.'" He shook his head and smiled. "I'm disappointed in you, Amber Catalina."

A bell jingled as the main door opened. The FBI agent entered, and the boisterous talking quieted to a hush. His figure was imposing, and for the first time, Jake felt like the man looked familiar. He was perhaps a few years younger than his parents, and his face was stern and unreadable. The dining hall host asked the man a question, and he answered by holding up two fingers. He went to the coffee pot, poured himself some coffee, and took a seat at a long table where he sat alone. Wes leaned across the table and whispered, "I wish I had one of those FBI jackets. They're so cool."

The dinner conversation returned to normal. Then the bell above the door rang again. A tall man with dark hair stood in the sunlit doorway. After glancing around, he crossed the room. Jake's eyes took a few seconds to adjust from looking into the bright sunlight. He could now see the man's blue FBI jacket. He sat down across from the other agent.

Wes leaned forward and whispered, "There's *two* of them now."

"Whatever's going on, it must be serious," Amber said. "I mean, you don't send the FBI down into the Grand Canyon when someone goes missing."

"You're right," Jake replied. "They'd send search and rescue and rangers—not FBI agents."

"When I talked to the ranch manager," Amber added, "she said that search and rescue has been looking for Agate since sometime last week."

Wes whispered, "My dad said that the FBI gets involved if there's some kind of federal crime that's been committed or if a fugitive is on the loose."

"They must think she did something pretty terrible." Amber's eyes narrowed. "Do you think she's dangerous?"

"No," Jake shook his head. "My grandpa trusted her. He must have because his letter says that we need to find her." He looked up at the ceiling again. "And I know where she's hiding."

Chapter 19

1880

Nahmida held Abe back against the rock. He could feel the boy's chest rise and fall as he took in another deep breath. The sound of the last gunshot still rang in their ears. Nahmida looked Abe in the eyes. "When I say, we run like lightning. You ready?"

Abe replied with a quick nod. The boy's eyes were resolute as cold steel.

"Now!"

The boys bolted across the narrow strip of sand and dove into the water. They swam as deep as they could. Dull booms of gunfire erupted overhead. But the current pulled their bodies downstream, around a river bend, and away from the men. Nahmida, the better swimmer, latched on to Abe's forearm and pulled him toward the sky. Bursting to the surface, the boys gasped for air.

"This way," Nahmida signaled toward the canyon wall. Abe plunged after him. The growing rumble of approaching rapids traveled across the water and into their ears. Abe looked at Nahmida with panic in his eyes.

"We're almost there," Nahmida said. "Relax, let the river do the work."

The flow pulled the boys alongside the dark canyon wall until they could feel stones and gravel under their feet. In front of them, an underwater ledge stretched out into the river. Diving forward, Nahmida launched toward the shelf. After two strong strokes, he pulled his knees to his chest and planted his feet upon its gritty surface. With a firm place to stand, he reached for Abe's hand and pulled him out of the current. Abe sat on the rock shelf in the shallow water, drawing in deep gulps of oxygen.

"I'm sorry," Abe said, "for almost getting you killed. You didn't have to..." He took in another deep breath.

"I didn't *have* to," Nahmida replied. "I *wanted* to. I've been treated like you've been treated, like a problem, like a fire that needs to be stamped out. In that way, we are brothers."

With the sounds of gunfire gone, the boys soaked in the quiet flow of the river. Behind them, the waters of a turquoise creek flowed from a narrow ravine into the dark waters of the Colorado River.

Nahmida signaled toward the blue-green waters. "Welcome to my home."

Chapter 20

The Hideout

After the sun had set and stars glimmered in the clear summer sky, Jake, Amber, and Wes crept from their cabins. Passing under the fluttering shadows of the great cottonwood trees, they made their way to the darkened canteen building. All Jake could hear were the sounds of the night wind rustling through the tall grass and the quaking of leaves overhead. A draft of cool air flowed like an invisible stream through the canyon.

"Jake, I'm not sure about this," Wes said.

"Our parents said we could explore," Jake answered. "as long as we stay between the ranch and the bridges."

"But they didn't say we could explore *at night*?"

"They also didn't say we couldn't," Amber added.

"Okay," Wes mumbled.

"This way," Jake said, edging around the building toward the back. "This is where I saw the light last night. And whoever was back here somehow climbed up onto the roof here." He pointed to the low roofline.

"I've got an idea," Wes said. "I thought I saw an old shed"—his voice began to trail off—"with stuff in it over here."

Wes disappeared into the darkness. A few seconds later came the clatter of things falling, followed by several grunts. Jake cringed. And then Wes emerged from the underbrush with a plastic five-gallon bucket. "Sorry about all the noise," he said, wincing with embarrassment. "I got into a fight with a couple of rakes and a shovel. Anyway, I thought we could use this as a step stool." He flipped the bucket upside down on the ground.

Amber stepped onto it and reached for the roofline, pulling herself up in one smooth motion. Jake followed, pulling with all his strength and then hooking his heel onto the asphalt-shingled roof. He started to fall backward when Amber grabbed his arm and shoulder. Stabilized by her grip, he lurched forward onto his belly and inched onto the roof.

Wes stood on the bucket, looking up at both of them. "I'm just going to stay down here."

"Come on, you can do it," Amber replied.

"If it was that hard for Jake to get up there, then I'm going to need some serious help."

"We've got you," Amber said. And she and Jake helped Wes safely onto the roof.

Jake walked up to the window and tugged on the frame. To his surprise, it slid right open. From the window, they had to step down into a room not much bigger than Jake's bedroom back at home. But in the dim moonlight, it was almost impossible to make out anything in the space.

Jake flipped on his headlamp. A camping mattress lay on the floor in the corner with a sleeping bag on top. Beside it was a stack of books. Under the opposite window were a small desk and chair. And on the desk sat an old ham radio, similar to the one in his grandpa's attic. A thin cable led from the device across the table and underneath the closed window casement. Someone had attached a corkboard to the wall, and upon it were several maps and notes pinned to it.

"Hey, Jake, shine your light over here," Amber said. "In the corner."

The rays of the headlamp landed upon coiled ropes and a climbing harness, as well as other gear that Jake couldn't identify, but he was sure had to do with rock climbing.

"It's got to be her," Amber said. "This is where she's hiding."

"Should we tell the agents?" Wes asked.

"No."

Jake froze. The voice didn't belong to Amber or Wes.

Jake swung the beam of his headlamp toward the window behind him. Between them and their exit stood a young woman. She looked exactly like the girl on the poster.

"I'm not missing," she said. "I'm hiding. And, Jake, I need your help."

Chapter 21

In the Attic

"Turn off your light, now," the girl demanded. "Or they'll find us."

Jake quickly reached up and switched off his headlamp. As his eyes adjusted to the darkness, her face became visible in the moonlight. When he'd first seen her photograph on the missing person poster, he'd thought she was pretty. Now standing here in front of him, with solemn eyes and her commanding presence, she was strikingly beautiful.

"Um," Jake stammered, "You know my name?"

"Of course, I know your name," she said. "Get down." Agate sat on the floor and motioned for the kids to do the same. "We don't want them to see movement up here."

"Why are you hiding?" Jake asked. "And why is the FBI after you?"

"They're actually after the *real* missing person—my dad," she replied. "He was supposed to meet you here, but he vanished. It happened about a month before the Marmot—I mean, your grandpa—passed away." Her eyes fell to the floor and she sighed. "They think I know where my dad is. And if they capture me,"—she edged onto her camp mattress —"they'll use me as leverage to draw him out of hiding."

"The agents?" Wes asked.

She nodded. "They first came last week disguised as rim-to-rim hikers. That's when I faked my disappearance. I would have just left, but I needed to stay for your arrival."

"To help us figure out the third clue?" Jake asked.

"Exactly," she replied. "When my dad disappeared, your grandpa sent me a message, telling me to meet you here. Anyway, those two men disguised as hikers left a few days ago —and returned posing as FBI agents."

The three kids stared at her in stunned disbelief.

"They're *posing*?" Wes asked.

"Yes," she answered. "Did you think that just because they have cheap-looking blue jackets with *FBI* printed on the back that they were legit?"

"Well, yeah," Wes replied. "I guess we...kinda...did."

"Well, it's possible they might be for real," she continued. "This whole thing goes deep—deeper than you or I can imagine. My dad and your grandpa believed that the Director already infiltrated intelligence agencies and bribed real agents. All I know for sure is that those guys in the blue jackets are bad."

Wes made a hooting sound, "Whooo, whooo, who, whoooo."

It took a second for Jake to realize the meaning of Wes's

sounds, but when he did, he held his head in his hands. "How did we miss it? Those FBI agents are—"

Wes finished Jake's sentence, "The Twin Owls."

"The twin *who*?" Agate asked.

"That's funny," Wes snickered. "You just said 'who' like an owl."

Agate didn't see the humor in Wes's attempt at a joke and stared back at him, waiting for the answer.

"They've been following us," Wes replied. "The first time we saw them was at Rocky Mountain National Park, at a place called the Twin Owls. That's how we named them. And then they showed up at the sand dunes trying to steal some artifacts."

"The arrowhead?" Agate asked.

"How did *you* know?" Amber replied.

Agate pointed to the ham radio on the desk. "At night, I connect a cable to the old trans-canyon telephone wires. Makes for a powerful antenna." She looked at Jake. "Your grandpa had a team. And they're still out there, rooting for you, Jake."

Jake felt that familiar thrum in his chest, the one that came when he thought of his grandpa, and that he'd trusted him to continue his quest.

"Down here in the canyon, there's no cell signal," Agate explained. "And Sat phones—that's what we call satellite phones—don't work half the time. Plus, it's safer. I'm sure my cell has been compromised. And if you three have phones, they probably have been, too."

Amber pulled her phone from her pocket. "Like my photos, GPS, text messages?"

"*Everything*," Agate replied. "But you're safe until you get back in cell range. Delete anything you don't want them getting."

"The clue from the gauging station," Jake said.

"I'm deleting it now," Amber replied. The screen illuminated her face as she scrolled through her photos and deleted the clue.

"Be careful how you use it," Agate added. "Searches, phone calls, anything. On this scavenger hunt, technology may not be your friend. Use it only when it's absolutely necessary."

Amber held the button on her phone, and its screen went dark.

"Wait," Wes screwed up his face in confusion. "How could the Twin Owls have been at the sand dunes last week, and here at the Grand Canyon looking for you?"

"Because there's more than just two," Agate answered. "They often work in small teams of two or three, but there's a whole troop of these guys."

"You mean, a *parliament*," Wes interjected.

Everyone looked at Wes like he was crazy.

"That's what you call a group of owls," he explained. "A *parliament*. A *troop* is what you call a bunch of baboons."

Agate's stern face brightened with a smile. "Maybe you should call them the *Twin Baboons*."

Wes laughed a loud laugh, then quickly covered his

mouth and cringed. “Sorry,” he whispered from behind his hand.

“Your grandpa said that your brother and friends might join you, but he didn’t mention their names.”

“Oh, yeah. Sorry, I totally forgot. “This is my cousin—”

“I’m Wes.” He leaned forward on his knees to shake her hand.

“And I’m Amber.”

“It’s good to meet you.” Agate sat back and smiled. “You guys already know my name from the posters, but just call me Agate. And I’m glad there’s four of us because it’s going to be close to impossible to get out of here without those guys capturing me or following you.”

She turned back to Jake, her eyes serious. “My dad should have sent you a package.”

“A package with an old wooden box in it?” Jake replied.

“That’s the one.”

“Your dad is...Mather?”

She nodded her head slowly. “Isaiah Albright. Code-name: Mather. And it’s good news those agents are after *me*, Jake. That means they think my dad still has the box. That’s what they really want. Whatever he did to get it to you must have worked.”

“Do you know what’s inside the box?” he asked.

She shook her head from side to side. “I don’t even think my dad knew. As a kid, I always wanted him to just break it open. But he would say, ‘It will open for the right person at the right time.’”

"That's almost exactly what my grandpa said in his letter, that it would open at the right time."

"And it's more valuable than all the treasures your grandpa and my dad discovered."

Jake leaned forward and his eyes grew wide. "Did you just say *treasures*? Like the plural of treasure?"

Agate nodded. "On their journeys, my dad and your grandpa found all kinds of stuff: old gold bars, silver, lost trunks, bags of cash, even paintings."

Jake shook his head in disbelief. Wes rolled onto his back, let out a long sigh and said, "I think my brain is going to explode."

"How about Long Tom's treasure?" Amber asked.

"They found that one in 2000," Agate replied, "just before I was born."

Jake's mind was spinning. "So, where did they hide all of it?"

"Only your grandpa knew."

The room fell silent. A rush of wind trembled the cottonwood leaves outside the window.

"We need to help you get out of here," Jake said. "We can't let them capture you."

"That's problematic," Agate replied. "I can't just leave. You're going to need my help to get to the last clue."

"The granary at Havasupai Gardens?" Wes asked.

"Yes, I've finally located it. It's near the Gardens, but not in it. And it's almost impossible to see without climbing. Definitely impossible to get to without ropes. It's at least a one-hundred-and-fifty-foot lead climb. I'm going to need a climbing partner to belay me."

"I can do that," Amber said.

Jake's annoyance crept in again. He knew Amber was the right person to do it. She was the more experienced climber. Once again, he was stuck in second place.

"How about the next clue?" Wes asked.

"Well, that's where things get a bit more complicated," Agate said. "Your grandpa didn't hide any of these pieces. Someone else hid them a long time ago. In his message, he told me what he knew. It's taken me a while to figure it out, but I'm pretty sure it's in cabin number nine. And that's a real problem."

Jake's brow furrowed. "Why is that a problem?"

Wes answered the question. "Because cabin number nine is where the"—he made air quotes with his fingers—"so called *FBI* agents are staying."

"You've got to be kidding me!" Jake grabbed his hair in his hands.

Agate looked at him, her eyes dead serious, "They're after me, sure. But they're also shadowing you." She pointed at Jake.

"Me?"

Agate's eyes shot to the ham radio. "I've been talking with the others at night. And the Director knows who you are, Jake. And he somehow figured out that your grandpa gave you something important, something that's leading you on this quest. I don't think he knows *what* it is. But he's tagged you. Not Amber, or Wes. He's shadowing you."

Jake tried to swallow the lump in his throat, but it wouldn't leave.

Agate continued, "So, in order to get the next two clues, we need to get rid of those agents."

Wes's mouth fell open. "You mean...*kill them*?"

Agate laughed. "Of course not, Wes. We just need to send them on a wild goose chase.

"How would we do that?" Jake asked.

"We let them find me," Agate replied.

"No way." Jake shook his head. "We can't risk you getting captured."

"It's the only way," she replied. "And I have a plan."

Chapter 22

The Plan

The next morning, Jake woke up first and met Amber outside at the picnic table. "I talked with Agate," Amber said. "And everything is a go." They reviewed the plan, and then Jake headed back to wake Wes.

He jostled his cousin. "It's time."

Wes rubbed his eyes and sat up. "Okay...okay...I'm up. Where are the red pandas?"

"Hey, Wes." Jake patted his cousin on the shoulder. "I don't think you're awake yet."

"Oh..." Wes shook his head. "I...I...was dreaming we were at the zoo being chased by these weird wolf-like things."

"We've got to get moving," Jake explained. "Amber already left to get Agate's bug-out bag."

"Did Agate's message go through?" Wes asked.

"It did," Jake smiled. "Amber said that she was able to

make contact with her friend, and the rafts will be at the beach in thirty minutes."

Wes, who had slept in his clothes, threw off his blankets, and walked to the door. Before grabbing the door handle, he turned to Jake and put out his fist. "Okay, I'm going to go find the ranch manager." He paused with his fist outstretched. "Don't leave me hangin' man. It's bad luck."

Jake turned, gave Wes a fist bump, and his cousin shot out the door.

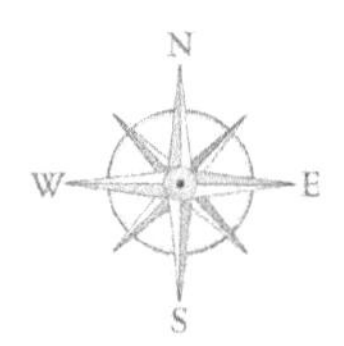

On the roof of the canteen, Jake climbed into the window to Agate's hideout. She stood beside the opposite window, securing a thick belt around her waist.

"What's that?" he asked.

"It's an inflatable PFD belt," she explained.

Jake gave her a blank stare.

"A personal flotation device. You pull this"—she pointed to a small, yellow plastic handle—"and it triggers the CO2 cartridge inside that fills up the life vest."

"That's cool," Jake said. "Are you sure you're going to be safe?"

"I'm not *sure*. But I'm confident. If I can swim out to the raft while it's *in the current*, we can put some distance between me and the agents." She pulled on a dusty, red ball cap—the same one from the missing person poster—and tied a red bandanna around her neck. "And climbing down from this window is tough. That will slow them down, too." She looked at her watch. "If Wes found the ranch manager, then the agents should arrive soon. You know what to do, right?"

Jake nodded. "When they come through the window, you'll go out that one." He pointed to the window on the opposite side of the room that now stood open. "And then I'll..."

The sound of voices rose from the ground below. "This is where I saw her, back here."

It was Wes's voice.

"And she climbed up there, and then went up into that window."

Jake hid in the corner of the room.

"I'll fetch you two a ladder," a voice said. Jake supposed it was the ranch manager.

Agate looked at him and winked.

Amber scrambled down the steep crag behind the gauging station. Her jump was smooth, and her feet landed with a solid thump on the strip of sand at the base of the tower. Tugging on the door they had loosened yesterday, she slipped through. This time she had her headlamp, and she found the bag right where they had left it. After slinging it over her shoulders, she made her way back down the rusty ladder rungs. She had ten minutes to get to Silver Bridge. The plan would only work if Agate had her gear.

From the tower, Amber hiked past Black Bridge and the ruins. The trail hugged the tan sands of the beach. It was still empty. The rafts had not yet arrived. She looked at her watch, and her stomach tightened with nervousness. *Where are they? They have to make it on time.* She set her eyes to the Silver Bridge and ran. At the bridge, she walked into the middle and turned to face upstream. From her new vantage point, she spotted three blue rafts slowly drifting toward the beach.

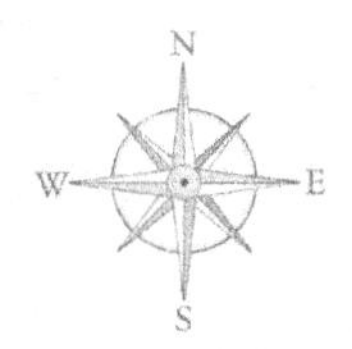

"Thanks for your help, young man," the ranch manager said, patting Wes on the back.

"You're welcome," Wes replied. "Well, I should get going and find my friends." He walked out to the main trail, and once he was out of sight, he sprinted down the path toward the river. He arrived just as the rafts slid onto the sandy half-moon beach.

"Bryce!" Wes called out. "I'm looking for Bryce."

"That's me," a guy in his early twenties held his hand up. He wore a beat-up straw cowboy hat, and a pair of sunglasses hung around his neck.

Wes checked his watch. "She'll be here in, like, five minutes," Wes said.

The guide turned to his crew. "Sorry, guys. We've got to launch now!" He pointed to the other two crews. "Boats two and three, things are going to get a little rowdy here soon. You're going to have two men who want to get in your rafts and follow us. Let them aboard. Just do whatever you can to keep a hundred yards between you and us. That's all we'll need."

"Julie,"—he pointed to a girl about Agate's age and height—"you'll be riding with me. Jump on in." A young woman in her early twenties stepped off the beach and into the lead raft with Bryce.

"Thanks, mister," Wes said, and then took off running toward Silver Bridge.

Jake could hear the men grunting and groaning as they pulled themselves onto the roof. A shadow flashed across the window panes. He could hear the window frame slide in its sash. A booted foot stepped through the opening and onto the floor. "She's here!" the man yelled to his companion.

Agate burst out the other window, but the man caught her foot. She slammed into the narrow ledge of the roof. He wrenched her ankle, and she cried out in pain. Jake's heart was beating in his throat. It took everything in him to stick to the plan and stay hidden in the corner. The second man entered through the window frame just as Agate kicked herself loose. Jake silently slipped out the other window without being seen. He carefully slid it shut. Then he jammed a piece of wood along the top to lock it in place, forcing their exit onto the other side.

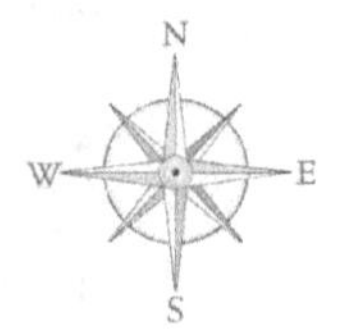

Amber watched from the bridge as one of the blue rafts launched from the beach into the slow-moving water. Then a flash of red curly hair caught her attention. Sprinting along the shore, Wes cut through a patch of knee-high grass to gain the path leading to Silver Bridge. She had never seen Wes move that fast. After pounding across the bridge, he arrived wheezing. Wes grabbed his knees, and tried to catch his breath.

The raft continued to drift toward the bridge. Amber could hear the guide directing his crew to row backward in an attempt to slow the boat down. Wes checked his watch. "She needs to get here quick," he said. "If she doesn't swim out before the bridge, she's not going to make it." Amber could hear the sound of rapids downstream behind her.

"It's going to work," Amber replied. "She'll make it."

But Agate was nowhere in sight.

Meanwhile, the slow, unyielding current was winning, pulling the raft along faster and faster toward the bridge and the rapids beyond it.

"There she is!" Wes pointed down the trail coming out of Bright Angel Canyon.

Agate dashed alongside the river, kicking up gravel behind her as she ran. One of the agents was right on her heels.

"The way she's running," Wes said, "she looks hurt."

The front of the boat began to pass below them, into the shadow of the Silver Bridge.

"Oh, no!" Wes said. "What is she doing? She's not going to the water! She was supposed to jump in the river and swim."

"It's too late, Wes. The boat's gone too far, and that

agent is too close. If she jumps in, he'll catch her." Amber picked up the pack, shouldered it, and turned to face downstream.

At that very moment, Agate's feet hit the bridge and she sprinted toward them.

"Drop it!" she yelled. "Amber, drop it!"

Amber slipped the pack off her shoulder, lifted it over the bridge railing, and let it go. She watched as it sailed through the air and splashed into the river. As soon as it hit the water, the river guide reached out and pulled it into the raft.

Agate's footfall rang out as she dashed down the bridge, followed by the thundering footfall of the agent. Then she did something that was definitely not part of the plan. In one swift move, she launched herself over the railing and jumped.

Stunned, the agent stared over the barrier, mouth agape. Amber and Wes watched with him as Agate plunged into the water, swam to the raft and climbed in. She turned, waved, and tipped her red ball cap at the agent. He spun around and began sprinting back toward the beach.

"I think it's working," Wes said, holding his fist against his teeth.

The agent soon joined his partner, who was already at the beach talking with the remaining boat crews.

Amber and Wes watched anxiously. "Get in," Wes murmured. "Just...get...in."

As if moved by Wes's words, the agent who'd chased Agate jumped into one of the boats and began yelling at the crew, "Row! Now! We have to catch them!"

In his excitement, Wes threw his hand out to give Amber a high five.

She shook her head and whispered, "Put your hand down. We can't let them suspect *anything.*"

"Oh. Yeah." He dropped his hand to his side. "Sorry."

Amber stared at the second agent, who still stood on the beach talking to the guide of the third raft. The guide beckoned him to join them. The agent shook his head, said something Amber couldn't make out, and then turned to walk back toward Phantom Ranch.

Wes looked at her in silence, his mouth open and eyes wide. "Oh, no. This is bad. Really, really bad."

"Come on. We've got to warn Jake," Amber said. They sprinted as fast as they could back toward the ranch.

Chapter 23

Cabin #9

After locking the two agents inside Agate's hideout, Jake snuck into the brush alongside the trail. A few minutes passed before the first man ran by, followed moments later by the second, both in pursuit of Agate. The plan was working. As soon as the men disappeared down the trail, Jake ran to cabin nine, opened the door, and slipped inside.

The space was slightly larger than the boys' cabin. A stone fireplace had been built in the corner, and two perfectly made twin beds were placed against the wall.

"Stand in the doorway," Jake murmured to himself. "The room will tell you." That's what Agate had told him: *The room will tell you the location of the third tile.*

He stood still with his back to the door, scanning the room and trying not to focus on any one object. The walls were built of large cobbles of round river rock, some light pink and orange, others dark gray or almost red in color. The sun filled the room with bright light, so bright Jake had to squint. Closing his eyes, he drew in a deep breath. The space smelled like cold stone, mildew, and old wood. Opening his eyes again, he took it all in. *The room is the clue.* He could feel his heart beating against his chest. If the plan worked, he would have plenty of time. Agate would swim out to the raft, and the agents would follow. They would end up miles downstream before they realized they'd been tricked. And they'd have no easy or quick way back to Phantom Ranch.

Jake tried to relax by closing his eyes again. As soon as they blinked shut, he saw it—an afterimage of the wall. Everything was in reverse. The light-colored stones were dark, and the dark ones were light. A pattern appeared.

He stared at the wall, straining to keep his eyes open wide. This time, when he closed his eyes, the afterimage pattern came into focus. The stones spelled something. His eyes flashed open, and he ran to the wall, where he began tracing the pattern of the lighter stones.

The first was the letter *F*, or maybe an *E*. It was hard to tell because a thick baseboard lined the bottom of the wall and covered some of the stones. The second letter was either an *I* or an *L*. Again, the baseboard made it difficult to read. Because some of the stones were larger than the others and protruded above the board, he decided it must be an *L*. The third pattern of stones looked to be an *I*. The fourth was the same. And the final letter appeared to form an *F*, or perhaps an *E*. Jake wanted to rip the baseboard off the wall so that he could see what had been hidden behind it.

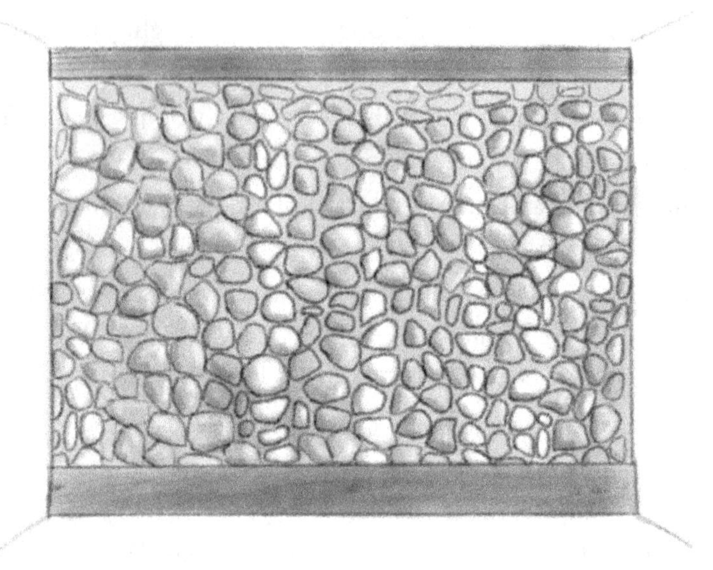

On the bedside table, he found a pad and pencil and wrote down what he had figured out so far: *F/E I/L I I F/E.*

He was grateful they had spent so much time figuring out the Mather Point clue. The practice helped his brain shift quickly into puzzle-mode. He began sketching out the possibilities.

None of them made any sense. Jake sat on the bed and tapped the pencil against the notepad. If only he could see the stones behind the baseboard. He wished he had a flashlight to shine into the gap between the wall and the board. Then, perhaps he could make out the darker stones from the lighter ones.

A knock came at the door. Jake sat bolt upright and held his breath.

"Housekeeping." It was a woman's voice. "I have fresh linens."

Jake cracked the door open to see the woman's face smiling back at him. She handed him a stack of white sheets and towels.

"Thank you," he said, and closed the door. Breathing a sigh of relief, he set the pile of linens on the bed by the window. The bright sunlight bounced off the white sheets, casting a soft glow onto the nearest section of the wall. *That's it!* The idea struck him like a jolt of electricity.

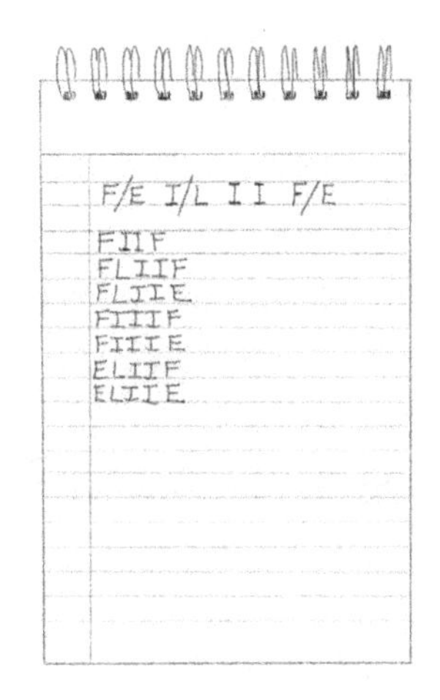

He ran to the bathroom and took the small framed mirror off the wall. Back in the bedroom, he stood above the baseboard and aimed the light from the mirror into the gap between the baseboard and the wall. It wasn't nearly as bright as a flashlight, but it worked. He could clearly see the darker stones from the lighter ones.

The first letter had no light stones at its base. It was definitely an *F*.

The second had a row of lighter stones, making it not a letter *I*, but a letter *L*.

What Jake had thought were two letter *I*'s, turned out to be connected by a line of lighter stones. It wasn't two letters —it was a single letter *U*.

The final letter had a line of lighter stones along the bottom. It was not an *F* but an *E*.

The word was clear: FLUE.

He'd only heard that word a few times. *It's an opening in a fireplace.* Jake spun around to face the stone fireplace. His grandparents' house had a similar one. Inside its firebox, he should find a metal handle to open and close the flue's damper door. Reaching inside, he felt around until he found it. Jake pulled, and the metal creaked. Ash and soot spilled onto the floor. The fireplace had not been used in many years. Reaching his hand into the flue, he began hunting until his fingers bumped something small and metal. He stretched his fingers but couldn't grasp it. Scooting closer, he plunged his arm further up and into the flue, found the object again, and wrapped his hand around what felt like a small, but heavy, jewelry box.

His arm was covered in black soot and red rust streaks, but in his blackened hand was all that mattered: an iron box.

Jake gripped the top and held his breath. He pried it open and peered inside. At the bottom was another small wooden tile with markings that matched the cube. He let out a long sigh of relief.

Just then, voices shouted from outside. He snapped the box shut.

It sounded like Wes and Amber, but he couldn't make out what they were saying. Frozen in place, he listened.

The voices called again, "Run! Jake! Run!"

He launched to his feet, and just as he reached for the door handle, it swung wide open. The agent stepped in and threw the door closed behind him. His eyes shot to the box in Jake's hand. He snatched it, opened the box, and dumped the tile into the palm of his hand.

Opening the door, he said, "You're going to leave, kid. And don't even try to accuse me of stealing from you." He laughed through his nose, like a bull snorting.

Jake didn't know what to do. The man tossed the soot-covered box back to Jake.

"It would be your word," the man added, "against an official from the FBI."

"There's nothing *official* about you," Jake stammered.

The agent smirked. "I'm sure they'll believe some thirteen-year-old brat, especially if I explain how you broke into my cabin." He gestured toward the door. "Get out."

Jake was frozen and speechless. He could see Wes and Amber standing outside, their red faces aghast. Defeated, he stepped over the threshold and out the door.

"Hey, kid."

Jake turned to face the agent.

"While you were helping us find this piece"—he held up the tile in his hand—"I found this." He reached into his jacket pocket and pulled out a wooden object. It was the cube—Jake's wooden cube.

Jake's heart stopped beating. The door slammed in his face.

Chapter 24

1880

Nahmida and Abe climbed onto a pink rock ledge and watched the blue-green water course through the narrow ravine.

"How far to your people?" Abe asked.

"We live in the valley past the three waterfalls." Nahmida pointed upstream and then looked at the sky. "We should make it in time for dinner." He beckoned Abe forward and slipped into the cool water.

The boys swam against the gentle current. Compared to the tow of the mighty Colorado, this creek relieved their spirits and settled their hearts. Since his youth, Nahmida had played in and explored every inch of Havasu Creek. He knew every rock and every tree like they were an extension of his family and his tribe.

Nahmida led Abe onto the sandbars to scramble over boulders polished smooth by centuries of flowing water. At times, the trail followed close against the ravine's walls, allowing them to travel faster on foot. When the path ended, they dove back into the deep emerald pools of the creek. At a tumbling cascade, the boys climbed the sleek, pink rock like a set of stairs coursing with water.

"You go ahead," Nahmida said, waving Abe past him.

As Abe crested the top of the cascade, the first waterfall came into view. He stood still, water pouring over his feet. Above them long, flat pools of turquoise water spilled one into the next in a series of small waterfalls. Abe gasped in wonder. Nahmida smiled at his response. "Come, friend," he said, tugging Abe's elbow. "It gets better."

Red flowers sprouted out of cracks in the rock, and cacti grew from the south-facing sides of the ravine. As the narrow gorge widened, trees pushed through the rocky soil. At first, the trees were small, scrubby things, but they grew taller as they moved deeper into an enormous side canyon. Their hands pressed against cool and spongy moss that grew in the shade, and their feet gripped the chalky gravel and sand of the creek bottom.

In the distance, a low rumble reverberated through the canyon. Great cottonwoods swayed in the breeze, and the rumble soon grew to a thunderous roar. The confined channel of the creek broke into a tree-filled valley. And before them, two hundred feet up the canyon wall, the blue waters of the creek plunged over the cliffside, sailing through the air and into a deep, clear pool. Seeing it, Abe froze, and his mouth dropped open. "I've never seen anything… I'm…I'm without words."

Nahmida smiled, and the boys dashed toward the pool and dove in. The spray of the waterfall swirled like a mist, caught the light of the sun, and amplified every color, turning the world into an enchanted place.

"Does it have a name?" Abe asked, staring up at the sight.

"Mooney Falls," Nahmida said, shaking his head. "It is a bit ironic."

Abe squinted, giving Nahmida a curious look.

"About five years ago, a gold prospector named Mooney tried climbing up there along the falls"—he pointed toward the top—"and he fell. He didn't survive." Nahmida shook his head again. "There are too many like him, gone crazy for gold and silver."

Abe stared up at the waterfall in wonder. "I think it deserves a better name."

"Maybe, one day," Nahmida replied, "it will have its true name again."

Mooney Falls

"I can feel it," Abe replied, still gazing up at the falls.

"What do you mean?"

"Sometimes, when I'm in the mountains, or along a river, or in a place like this, I see it, but I also *feel* it. It's like hearing the voice of someone you know."

Nahmida smiled. "I understand." He tapped Abe on the chest. "You have a true heart, friend."

The boys found a stretch of rock and lay in the sun to warm themselves. The smooth surface radiated heat into their skin and dried their bodies.

Nahmida stood and rubbed his hands together. "We are halfway there."

After another hour of hiking alongside the creek, the canyon opened to a broad valley of pastures, fields of newly planted corn, and orchards of peach trees. The sound of children filled their ears.

"Nahmida!" a child's voice called. Nearly twenty people had come to greet them.

Chapter 25

Lost

Jake sat on the bottom bunk, holding his head in his hands. "I thought he was gone."

Wes and Amber sat on the bunk across from him, both without words.

"What happened?" He raised his head to meet their eyes. "The plan was for the agents to follow Agate in the rafts." Tears welled behind his eyes, and he took a deep breath in an attempt to hold them back.

"The first agent got in and left," Amber said softly. "And the second agent was on the beach with the other raft. We thought he was going to get in. Then, at the last moment, he waved them off and left the beach."

"We were still out on the Silver Bridge," Wes added, "kinda far away. When he left and started heading back, we bolted to get here. But he had a big head start. And then, it was like he just disappeared."

Wes went quiet.

"Why did I leave it here?" Jake grabbed his hair with clenched fists.

"Leave what?" Wes said, his face somber.

"Didn't you guys see?" Jake let go of his hair and looked at them with reddened eyes.

"We could barely hear what was going on in the agent's cabin or see anything."

"The cube, Wes," Jake answered. "Somehow, he got in here and stole *the cube*!"

"He did what?" Amber's face fell.

Wes exploded to his feet. "In here? He got in *our* stuff? And just took it?" He paced the small room and then turned around. "Who does he think he is?"

"They think they can do whatever they want," Amber began, "capture whoever they want, and *take* whatever they want."

"He has the third tile *and* the cube?" Wes jabbed his fingers into the curls of his hair.

Jake was silent but looked at his cousin and nodded.

Wes pressed his forehead against the bedpost of his bunk and let out a long *Aughhhhhh*.

It felt like all the blood in Jake's head was sinking into his stomach and throbbing in his legs. After a couple of minutes, he raised his head to find Amber looking at him.

"Are you gonna give up?" she asked.

Jake had to think about it. None of this was supposed to happen. The agents weren't supposed to win. Hopefully, Agate was safe, and the escape part of the plan worked. But what about Grandpa Evans? He'd invested so much to keep the clues safe and out of the hands of these men. A wave of anger rose in his chest. His shoulder muscles tightened, and what felt like a smoldering fire crept into his face. He narrowed his eyes and set his jaw.

"No. I'm not going to give up," he said.

"Good," Amber replied. Her eyes were resolute as steel. "I've got an idea. But—" she paused. "I'm not sure you want my help, Jake."

"What do you mean?" he asked.

"I mean, what we talked about the other day. Something's going on between us." Amber looked at him, waiting for a response. Jake felt like a deer in the headlights. His emotions were a tangled mess of twine impossible to unravel into words.

"You keep pushing me aside," she continued. "Everything I do, for some reason, you keep turning into a threat."

Jake's eyes dropped to the floor. Already defeated, he could feel his resistance crumbling. "Yeah...I guess you're right. I've just..." He hesitated, trying to find the words—the true words. "I've never had a friend who's good at everything —who's *better* at everything."

"That's not true," Amber replied.

"Yes, it is. You're faster. You're a better climber. You figure things out so quickly. When we bike, you're way better than me...and Wes."

Amber looked at Wes.

Wes shrugged and said, "He's right."

"And I guess," Jake continued, "I guess...it makes me feel like I'm no good."

That was it, the jumbled-up thing he didn't want to admit. But now that he said it, he was afraid of how Amber might respond. "I don't mean that you're trying to make me feel that way. It's like a reaction inside me. I keep trying to press it down, but then it explodes in my face. And I don't like it." Jake met Amber's eyes. "I'm sorry, Amber."

Amber looked down at the floor. "Thanks for saying that, Jake." Then she got quiet.

He guessed that she must be gathering her thoughts. Then she looked him straight in the eyes and said, "This might sound rough, but I'm not going to change who I am to make you feel better."

"And I don't want you to," Jake replied. "I guess I've got to figure out how to be okay with it."

"With *it*?" she asked.

"I mean, I have to figure out how to be okay with you being *you*," Jake answered.

Amber smiled. "That sounded honest. And true."

No one knew what to say. So, they sat in silence for a moment.

Then Wes clapped Jake on the back. "Now that you two settled all that, are we going to hear her idea?"

Jake bit his lip and nodded. "Yeah, let's hear it."

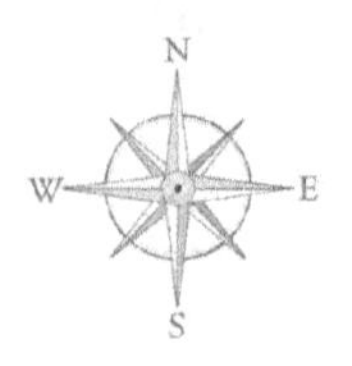

The raft shot a powerful run of rapids and then followed the current through a great bend in the river. Agate reached out and tapped Bryce on the shoulder. "This is the spot," she said.

As the river guide beached the raft, Agate gave her red cap and bandana to a girl named Julie, who was about her same size. Agate shouldered her wet pack and stepped onto the sandy strip.

Giving Bryce a hug, she adjusted the straps. "Thanks for getting me out of this." She glanced upriver. "You guys better get going. They'll be here soon."

Bryce stared up at the canyon wall. "Are you sure you can climb out of here?"

She smiled. "I'll be fine."

"This is how people die out here, Agate. Climbing rock like that solo."

"It's my only way out," she replied. "The path back to the plateau is just over that lower lip." She pointed to a jagged gap in the rock. Then she gave him a playful punch in the shoulder. "Now, you guys get out of here."

Bryce lowered his sunglasses and returned to the boat. "Let's head out!"

Agate dashed into a copse of willows to hide. Minutes later, the second raft drifted past. When they were out of sight, she began her climb.

Chapter 26

1880

Nahmida's friends and family embraced him and spoke his people's word of greeting, *gam'yu*. Several children tugged on Abe's strange and tattered clothing. Nahmida nudged Abe and pointed out two orange stone pinnacles that rose above the valley floor. "Those we call the *Wiï gl' iiva*, the Protectors of our home."

The boys and the villagers traveled a wide dirt path that cut its way through a meadow of summer grass where horses and mules grazed. Nahmida led Abe to an older man who sat in the shade of a pecan tree, resting from his labors and from the heat. Sitting down beside him, Nahmida began speaking in the language of his people. After a brief conversation, the older man reached out and shook Abe's hand.

"Abe, this is Hmaañ Gjaah, Guardian of the Children," Nahmida said. "He would like to see the object."

Abe pulled the cube from his pocket. He handed it to the man, who proceeded to turn it over, then shake it. Something inside rattled. After handing it back to Abe, Hmaañ Gjaah's face became grave, and he began speaking to Nahmida.

"He says he does not know what it means, but Gswedva will, for he is older and knows about such things." Nahmida nodded in respect to his elder, who appeared distracted, deep in thought.

"Something troubles him," Nahmida said to Abe and then began to ask Hmaañ Gjaah what was on his mind.

After several minutes of conversation, Nahmida explained, "The Haygu—outsiders—have found silver, and they intend to fence us in, to make our home a cage, and have told us we cannot return to our winter lands on the plateau. We cannot survive down here in the canyon during the cold months. There is no game to sustain us."

What Hmaañ Gjaah told Nahmida next filled him with fear and confusion.

"What is it?" Abe asked.

"The Haygu, they plan to take the children."

Abe's eyes narrowed, and his lips pursed. "Take the children?"

"They say the children must be educated elsewhere, learn new ways. But we don't believe them."

"What will you do?" Abe asked.

"We don't know," Nahmida replied. "But we will find a way." He rose to his feet. "We sleep in the village tonight. Tomorrow, we leave to find Gswedva."

Chapter 27

Amber's Idea

Wes sat back down on his bunk. "So, what's your idea?"

"Agent—I mean Owl—number two still needs the last tile," Amber explained. "That means he is going to follow us. And that's a good thing."

"How's that a good thing?" Wes asked. "I wish I would have bodychecked that guy on the bridge when he was running after Agate."

"Um, Wes," Jake said, "I think he would have just run you over."

Wes blew out a breath. "It would have been worth it. Then I would have taken his FBI jacket." Wes paused. "No, I wouldn't—that would be stealing."

"Anyway," Amber continued, "because he'll be at Havasupai Gardens, it gives us a chance to recover the cube and the tile he took from Jake."

Jake leaned in. "How do we do that?"

"So, for the Agents or Twin Owls, or whatever they are, Agate is the key to getting Mather," Amber explained. "And you"—she pointed at Jake—"are the key to *finding the last clue.*"

"I'm following you," Jake said.

"So, we need *you* to be the decoy while Wes sneaks in to recover the cube and the tile."

"Me?" Wes pointed at himself with his thumb. "I get to steal stuff?" He rubbed his hands together and got a crazed look in his eyes. "I mean...I don't like stealing stuff. That's not okay. But stealing stuff *back*, what's rightfully ours—that sounds splendid."

Jake laughed at his cousin, and Amber snickered. "Well,"—she let out a breath—"don't get too excited. This is going to be tough."

"First, we'll need a way for Jake to lure the agent away," Wes said. He pinched his chin, deep in thought. "I've got it! He threw his finger to the sky. We build it!"

"Build what?" Amber asked.

"We build the fourth clue," Wes explained. "We make a *fake* tile for our *fake* FBI agent." Wes looked at Amber and Jake, his eyes wild with excitement. "Back behind the canteen, in the trees, is a pile of old wood. And I've got this." He pulled out his pocket knife. "I'll carve a tile that looks just like one of the clues."

"Wes, that's perfect!" Amber gave him a fist bump.

"It's genius," Jake added. "I'll use the fake clue as bait to draw the agent away."

Amber nervously tapped her foot on the cabin's wood-planked floor. "Tomorrow, at Havasupai Gardens, you'll act like you're going off on your own to find the clue. He'll follow you. And you can then pretend to find it. He'll do the same thing he did today; he'll take it. And that will give Wes enough time to go through the agent's gear and get the cube and the third clue."

"What will you be doing?" Wes asked.

"I'll meet up with Agate, just like we planned," Amber answered. "And help her get the fourth clue from the granary."

"So, I'm just bait?" Jake asked.

Wes snickered.

"What?" Jake asked.

A grin lit up Wes's face. "I just imagined you as a worm, but with your face on it."

Jake rolled his eyes.

"It's the only way this is going to work," Amber explained. "They're not going to follow Wes or me. It's got to be you."

Then a thought came to Jake that had not occurred to him before. "I do like the idea of outsmarting that guy."

But when he said "outsmarting," he realized that it wasn't his idea. It was Amber's, and a jab of jealousy, like a bee sting, made his chest and throat tighten. Instead of holding it in, he decided to be honest.

"Amber, I'm feeling jealous." He paused for a second. "Because it's *your* plan. And because it's a really good one." Jake paused for a second, then blew out a sigh. "And because it's not mine."

He wasn't sure what to say next. The silence felt awkward. *This is why I hate saying what I'm feeling. I only end up feeling more stuff.* Embarrassment set his face on fire.

"Thanks," Amber replied.

Hearing just that one word, Jake's discomfort ebbed away.

"Seriously, Jake," Amber continued. "That's what I meant about being honest. If you bottle that up, I still feel it. But you saying it, it kinda..."

"Sets it free." Jake finished her sentence. And he could feel the jealousy evaporating like a shallow puddle in the heat of a Grand Canyon sun.

Wes sprang to his feet and put on his shoes. "I'm going to do some woodworking."

Jake smiled at his cousin. A whirlwind of emotions spun around inside him. Excitement and nervousness, grief and courage all swirled about. But the biggest thing he felt was relief, relief from the jealousy that had weighed him down like a backpack full of rocks. He drew in a deep breath, let it out, and felt his shoulders lift.

Tomorrow, they'd leave Phantom Ranch to camp at Havasupai Gardens, and have their chance to recover what was rightfully theirs.

Chapter 28

Havasupai Gardens

That night, Jake could barely sleep. He lay in his bed, staring at the wooden slats of the top bunk. They had a plan—but their first plan had failed. Agate had escaped, but he lost the cube. And if they failed to recover it, their quest would be over. Jake imagined the next month and a half wandering through beautiful places in solemn silence and a heart of regret. All the work his grandfather had done, the risks people like Agate and Mather had taken, would be wasted because he'd been outwitted by the Director and his goons.

His thoughts were pinging around inside him like a pinball machine. Who was the Director? Why was he after the clues? Where was he? Or maybe *he* wasn't a *he* after all. Maybe the Director was a *she*? And the agents. Were they fake? Or real FBI agents turned rogue?

He took some comfort in the fact that Agate was safe—at least, he hoped she was safe. Somewhere, she was out there, in the middle of the Grand Canyon under a starlit sky. He imagined her perhaps warming her hands over her camp stove. Jake's eyelids grew heavy, and his mind slowed. His thoughts gave way to dreams, and he fell asleep.

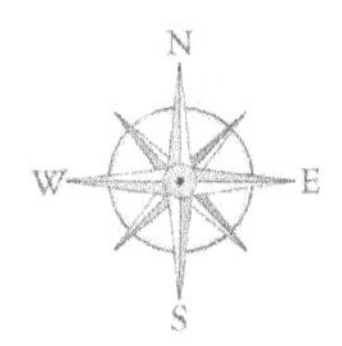

In the morning, the three families gathered for breakfast in the canteen. After thanking the ranch staff, they began their hike to Havasupai Gardens. The parents stopped at the Silver Bridge to take photos, giving Jake, Amber, and Wes the opportunity to put some space between them.

Wes pulled out the map and studied it. "Agate said to try the radio when we get to the top of Devil's Corkscrew."

"That sounds terrible," Amber said.

"It is terrible," Wes replied. "It climbs five hundred feet in half a mile. But at the top, the radio should work. If she made it."

The trail snaked along narrow ledges, dipping in and out of the shadows of the towering canyon walls as it followed Pipe Creek through the ravine.

"I didn't expect so much green," Jake said. "Or flowers." The creek was lined with low-growing willows, and vibrant blue and red wildflowers sprouted from the shallow edges of the creekbed.

About an hour into their ascent, the kids stopped in the shade of the River Resthouse, a stone and wood structure created along the banks of Pipe Creek. Jake read the interpretive sign near the structure: *Built by the Civilian Conservation Corps in the 1930s, the River Resthouse serves as a retreat from the sun and inclement weather for thousands of hikers each year.*

River Resthouse

Hikers had not only taken shelter under its roof, they had also carved their names into almost every exposed wood surface. "Jake, check this out," Wes called to his cousin.

Jake walked into the shelter, and Wes lifted a hinged surface that looked like a small desk. Inside was a notebook that read: *Pipe Creek Resthouse Visitor Register. Please sign in and share your thoughts.* Wes picked up the pen and began writing his name into the log.

That's strange, Jake thought to himself. *This place has two names.*

"From here, it's about three more miles to Havasupai Gardens," Amber said. "And it's all up." She stepped outside and pointed to the trail, which zigzagged up the side of the Grand Canyon. "This is going to hurt." Wes massaged his legs to get them ready for the climb. "Sorry, Jake, I'm not sharing my trekking poles this time."

"That's okay," Jake said after finishing a swig of water from his hydration pack. "I'm feeling good today. Just sweaty." He tugged on the front of his shirt, which was already sticking to his chest.

With her hand, Amber shaded her eyes from the sun and stared up at the impossible-looking path before them. "Alright, boys, let's do this thing."

Devil's Corkscrew was aptly named. The trail coursed through what felt like endless switchbacks along the side of a steep and rocky escarpment. Soon, the sound of clopping hooves caused the three kids to crane their necks and scan the trail above them. A mule train was snaking down the path, kicking up dust and carrying tourists from the rim.

"We need to get off the trail," Wes said.

Wes and Amber stepped to their right, toward the exposed edge of the path.

"Wrong way, guys," Jake said, scrambling up the inside of the trail. Jake had read a sign earlier that gave instructions for hikers encountering mules. "Remember what the sign said? We're supposed to go to the *inside* of the trail."

Wes and Amber hurried to join Jake. The lead wrangler tipped his cowboy hat and thanked the kids for allowing them the right of way. The clip-clop of the mules' hooves continued as the train navigated the switchback and made its way past. Then, one of the animals stopped right in front of them. The woman sitting on its back clenched the reins, and her mouth hung slightly open. "Why is he stopping?" the rider called out, a nervous quiver in her voice.

Jake peered over the rim side of the trail and immediately understood her concern. Sitting atop an animal on a path that overlooked a great plunge to the canyon below had to be unnerving.

"He's just making a little pit stop," the other wrangler answered from the rear of the caravan.

The mule proceeded to relieve itself right in front of Wes.

He scrunched up his face and said, "I want to make a poop joke right now, but I won't."

"Why not?" Jake asked. "It's never stopped you before."

"Because...it would probably just stink," Wes replied with a smirk.

Jake looked at the ground and shook his head.

"You stepped right into that one," Wes added.

Amber shook her head as the final mule passed. The kids stepped back onto the trail, and they soon reached the plateau above Devil's Corkscrew.

"We should have pretty good reception here," Wes said. "Try the radio."

Amber took off her pack and began digging to find the radio. At the same time, Jake borrowed Wes's pair of compact binoculars and surveyed the Devil's Corkscrew trail below them. "I can see the mule train," he said, "I'm pretty sure that group below the mules is our parents."

"How about the agent?" Wes asked.

"No sign," Jake replied. He continued scanning the long, twisting trail into the far distance. "Wait. I think that's him. Looks like he's a few minutes behind our parents."

The radio blared with static as Amber switched it on. She turned it to channel three, and pressing the call button, she spoke into it. "Agate, this is Amber; come in."

Static.

Amber repeated her words into the radio. More static. Then a garbled voice came through.

"I think it's her," Amber said. She held the speaker close to her ear. "But we might be too far away."

"Ten-one," Amber said. "Ten-one, over and out." She switched off the radio.

"Ten-one? I've heard of ten-four, but what does ten-one mean?" Wes asked.

"It means that the signal is bad," Amber explained. "So, if Agate could hear me, she'll know why I couldn't talk." She turned off the radio and handed it to Wes, who put it back in her backpack.

Above Devil's Corkscrew, the trail entered a tree-lined ravine carved from the ancient rock by the waters of Garden Creek. Jake led them down a spur trail to a small waterfall. The murmur and buzz of the cascades refreshed their spirits after the demanding ascent. The kids removed their boots and socks to soak their feet in the cool waters of the creek.

Wes wriggled his toes. "I sure hope she's okay."

"She's okay," Amber replied. "I can feel it. We'll try the radio again when we get to Havasupai Gardens."

Wes quickly turned his head and stared up at the rim of the gorge. "Did you guys see that?"

A bright glint of light flashed across Jake's body. "There it is again," Wes called out. "It's on you, Jake!" He pointed to his cousin's chest.

Jake saw the light glimmer on his shirt. In a flash, it disappeared. "What was that?"

"Whatever it was, it definitely came from up there," Wes pointed to the edge of the gorge.

Jake and Amber studied the rim, but all they could see were trees and plants rustling in the breeze. Wes dug into his backpack and appeared to be sketching and writing something into his notebook.

When they finished cooling off, the kids continued up Bright Angel Trail. The path wound through Garden Creek Canyon, hugging its sheer cliff walls.

"Just one mile to go," Wes said, tapping a trail sign with one of his trekking poles.

And thirty minutes later, they entered Havasupai Gardens. A pair of massive cottonwoods greeted them and formed an arch over the trail. Redbud trees lined the dirt path, and a broad, green valley opened before them. Canyon walls fenced in the meadows, creating a hidden oasis protected by rock and time.

"This place reminds me of Phantom Ranch," Jake said, spinning around to take it all in. "But bigger."

Following the campground signs, the kids located their sites and unpacked the small two-person tent for Jake and Wes.

While the boys began setting up the tent, Amber sat down at the picnic table and took off her backpack. The campsite was surrounded by small trees and shaded from the sun by a shelter that cast its shadow across the picnic table and tents. She dug around in her backpack and pulled out the radio.

"I'm going to try Agate again." She flipped it on and pressed the button. "Agate, this is Amber. Do you copy?"

Static.

"Agate, we are at Havasupai Gardens. Can you hear me?"

"Loud and clear, Amber," a staticky voice replied.

Wes and Jake dropped the tent poles they'd been assembling and ran to Amber's side.

The voice on the radio came through again. "And with my binoculars, I can see you, too."

"What's your twenty?" Amber asked.

"Your twenty?" Jake whispered with his brow knit.

"It means *location* in radio talk," Amber answered.

"Look to your east," Agate said.

Jake and Amber both looked at Wes, who had already pulled out his compass.

"She's that way," he said, pointing in the direction of the main trail.

They caught a brief flash of bright light in the distance. Agate was using a small mirror to signal her location. The glimmer of light was unmistakable, even though she was half a mile away.

"Meet me here. Tomorrow morning, at six forty-five. Over," Agate said.

"Affirmative. Over and out," Amber replied and turned off the radio.

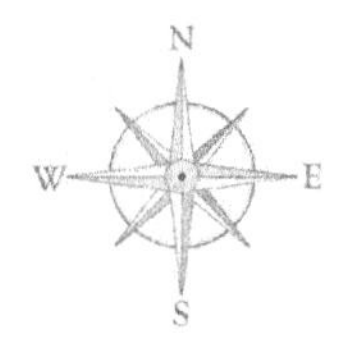

Their parents arrived shortly after noon and invited the kids to play a dice game in the shade of one of the shelters. All nine of them scrunched onto the long spruce boards of the picnic table. "It's going to be like Phantom Ranch," Uncle Brian began. "You kids are free to explore."

"We're planning to do some exploring in the morning," Jake replied.

"That's fine," Uncle Brian said. "Just be packed and ready to hike out at ten o'clock."

Wes had appointed himself lookout for the agent. About halfway through the second game, Jake noticed his cousin staring at something behind him. He pretended to stretch and looked over his shoulder. The agent was setting up camp, three campsites away, a hundred feet from the boys' tent.

After an early dinner, the kids retreated to an old stone shelter house to work out the details of their plan. A series of wide stone steps led down into the structure. They didn't want to be anywhere near the agent who might overhear them.

"This place is cool," Wes said as he unfolded the Grand Canyon map onto the table. He handed Amber his notebook and a pencil.

Jake was amazed at how many carvings people had etched into the wood: initials and dates, and some so old they were no longer legible. "It's kinda sad that people have done this. I mean, it's a historical building."

"Yeah, not cool," Wes replied.

Amber began to draw out the plan, so the boys shifted their attention from the hiker graffiti to the notebook.

"We're here," she said and drew a tent to signify their campsite. "And the agent is here." She drew another tent and an owl beside it. Consulting the Grand Canyon map, she marked a line representing the canyon walls that enclosed Havasupai Gardens. She sketched a line for the Bright Angel Trail and finished by drawing a compass rose.

"At six thirty, I'm going to leave and head up to where Agate is hiding near the granaries." She drew a capital *A* for Agate's location. "If something goes wrong, and you guys need to find us, look for this landmark." She drew an *X* on the location. "I scouted it out earlier. It's a big piece of rock that looks like it fell from the canyon wall." She began drawing a dashed line. "There's a hidden trail back there, and it will lead you to our location below the granaries."

"You're pretty good at drawing," Wes said.

"She's good at pretty much *everything*," Jake replied.

Amber looked at Jake. He could tell, from the look on her face, that she was concerned. Was Jake's jealousy going to get in the way?

"Don't worry," Jake said with a smile. "I'm just being honest."

Amber's shoulders relaxed, and she continued. "When I leave, that will be the signal for you guys"—she pointed the tip of the pencil at Jake and then Wes—"to start your part of the plan. If this works, the agent is going to follow you, Jake. And you'll lead him this way." She drew a dashed path onto the map. "Far away from me and Agate."

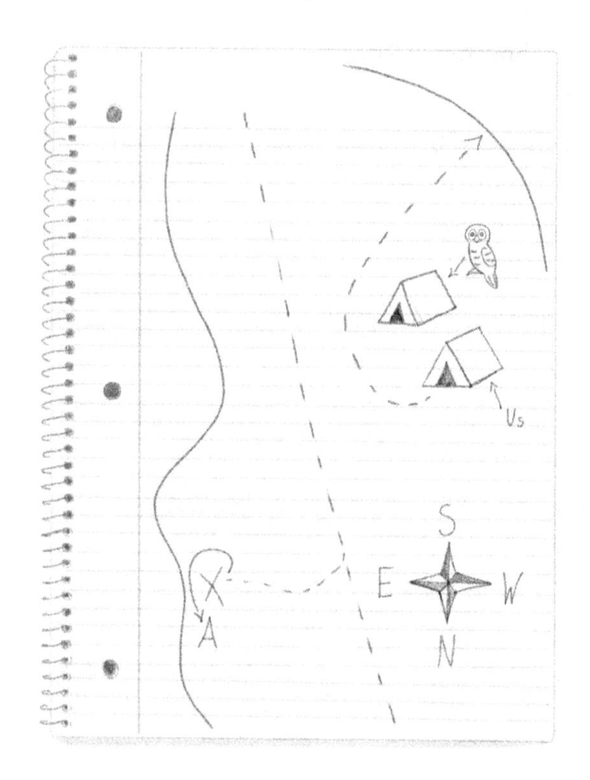

Wes pulled something out of his pocket and handed it to Jake. It was the square piece of old wood he had carved to look like one of the clues. "You'll need this."

Jake picked it up and turned it over. "This is amazing! It looks so legit."

"I rubbed it around in the dirt for a while to make it look old," Wes replied.

"Wes, you're going to stay put," Amber continued, "and pretend like you're still asleep in the tent."

"Oh, that will be easy," Wes said. "I'm pretty much a professional at sleeping."

Amber snickered. “When you see the agent leave, you can go find the cube and recover the third clue.”

“You mean *steal* them back,” he said. “This is totally like we’re in a heist movie. I love it.”

“While you guys distract the agent, I’ll belay Agate while she climbs up to get clue number four.”

“Belay?” Jake raised an eyebrow.

“*Belay* is a rock climbing term. Basically, it means I hold the rope and take up the slack as she climbs. If she falls, then I’m the one who keeps the rope locked off and secured.”

“What about the old couple?” Wes asked.

“Let’s just focus on the agent,” Amber replied.

“Well, I’m going to keep an eye on them.” Wes's eyes narrowed. “I still don’t trust them.” He rubbed his chin. “Hmmm, I think I’m going to need a Ziploc bag and some duct tape.”

“To do what?” Jake asked.

“Maybe nothing,” Wes said. “I’m thinking through my Plan B, just in case something goes wrong.”

Chapter 29

1880

Nahmida and Abe hiked for three days to *The Place Below the Spruce Trees.* They hoped to find Gswedva there. Late in the day, with the setting sun at their backs, the boys spotted the flickering orange glow of a distant campfire.

Nahmida pointed it out to Abe. “It is Gswedva and his family.” The boys could now make out shadows moving in the firelight.

The Place Below the Spruce Trees, like Supai Village, was a green, level place in the middle of an arid and rocky canyon. There were places where the earth was cultivated into gardens, growing beans, squash, and corn. A creek had been diverted to water the plantings. The fluttering leaves of tall cottonwoods were the only sounds that broke the silence of twilight. But soon, the boys heard voices, and Nahmida recognized Gswedva’s deep and resonant words of welcome.

The man was broad and tall, his hair jet black. His

imposing presence would have been intimidating if he hadn't been so friendly. Gswedva's eyes carried both years of concern and kindness.

"Who is your companion?" he asked in the language of Nahmida's tribe.

"This is Abe," Nahmida explained.

Gswedva nodded a greeting.

"I found him being hunted by Haygu along the north rim," Nahmida explained, pointing to the north.

The older man's eyes knit in concern. "Come, we have a meal ready, venison and corn." Gswedva gestured toward the light of the fire, and the boys followed him.

As the fading sun fell behind the canyon walls, Gswedva fed the fire, and the famished boys enjoyed their first real meal since they left Supai.

Gswedva looked across the fire to Nahmida. "You boys have come with a purpose. I can see it in your walk and hear it in your voice."

Nahmida smiled and looked at Abe. "Show him the object."

Abe handed the cube to Gswedva.

The man turned it over and examined it in the firelight. Smiling, he ran a fingernail along its edge, then gently grabbed one of its sides and twisted. The cube unlocked and opened on a set of invisible hinges. Inside was a stack of small wooden tiles. Gswedva motioned to Abe, who approached. He held the boy's hand and dropped the pieces into his open palm. Nahmida watched Abe count them: one, two, three, four, five, six.

Gswedva took the flattened cube and set it in the dirt. Taking the tiles from Abe, he began fitting them into their places around the cross.

Staring into the fire, Gswedva ran his fingers across his bearded chin, then spoke one word, "*Mukuntuweap*."

"What does it mean?" Abe asked.

Nahmida shook his head. "I've never heard the word before. It's not a word from our people."

Gswedva explained the meaning of the word.

"It is from the Paiute," Nahmida translated. "He says that it means *the canyon of the straight arrow*."

"Is he certain?" Abe asked.

Nahmida inquired.

Gswedva shook his head, then spoke in a low and serious tone.

"He said that only part of it is clear," Nahmida explained.

Gswedva pointed to the top of the cross and tiles. He repeated the word. "Mukuntuweap." Then he pointed to the bottom and again shook his head.

"To understand, you will need to go to the Paiute in Mukuntuweap," Nahmida said.

Abe mouthed the word. "Mukuntuweap."

Chapter 30

Decoy

Jake woke to beeps coming from Wes's watch alarm. It was 6:25 a.m., time to execute their plan. Wes, who was usually drowsy in the morning, was wide awake. Jake gave his cousin a silent fist bump, then crept out of his sleeping bag and unzipped the tent. Wes remained still and silent behind him.

When Jake stepped outside, he stole a glance at the agent's campsite. The man was already awake, reading something and sipping a steaming cup of coffee. Jake went to the picnic table and slowly began packing his daypack. He hoped the agent would notice. Jake glanced over again and saw the man had already slipped off his camp shoes and was hastily lacing up his boots.

Jake flung his pack over one shoulder and walked to the water spigot to fill his hydration bag. He could feel the eyes of the agent on his back the entire time.

Jake found a trail in the shallow wash west of the ranger

station. Distant footsteps crunched in the dry dirt behind him. Jake's body buzzed with jitters. He took in deep breaths to keep calm. So far, the plan was working.

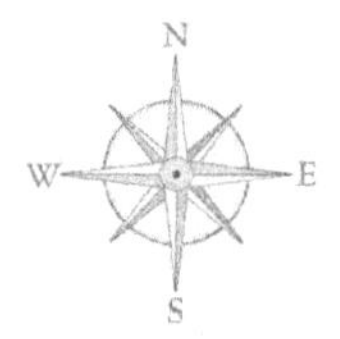

Wes could hear the agent scrambling around his campsite. Laying impatiently in his sleeping bag, Wes waited until the man left, then set his timer for ten minutes. That would give Jake time to lure the agent far enough away from the campground. Wes checked his daypack to make sure he hadn't forgotten anything and then slipped its straps over his shoulders. He watched the timer on his watch as it counted down, tension building in his chest with each passing second.

The timer on Wes's watch hit zero, and his hands shook with excitement and anxiety. He peered out of the tent and scanned the campground. All the nearby campsites were empty, or the campers were still asleep. After stuffing his hair into a ball cap, he slipped on his camp shoes and made his way to the agent's tent. He tried to walk quietly and dampen the crunching sound of the gravel under his feet. Looking over both shoulders, he unzipped the flap and crawled inside.

While Jake hiked west, Amber headed northeast along the Bright Angel Trail. She soon located the faint path leading east toward the looming cliffs of Garden Creek Canyon.

After the path became indiscernible, she followed the gravel bed of a steep gully as it curved toward the large broken rock that was her waypoint. Agate was somewhere up there, waiting for her.

Jake's path had also become steep. It took everything in him not to look back. He couldn't let on that he knew he was being followed. Pausing for a moment, he studied the distant canyon walls. He needed a spot, a convincing hiding place where he could pretend to find the fake clue. He rubbed the wooden tile in his pocket just to make sure it was still there.

He spotted a long, dark fissure that ran through the red sandstone cliffs, a jagged crack shaped like a lightning bolt. *That's the perfect place.* Setting his eyes on the dark feature, he adjusted his bearing and began to climb a long and narrow wash toward the base of the cliffs.

Jake let out a long sigh. He thought of Amber helping Agate, and of Wes recovering the items he had lost. *I'm a decoy, nothing more than a decoy.* Things were just as he had feared: he couldn't be trusted. Amber and Wes were better at everything. He wasn't leading. Just being followed.

Like the agent behind him and the wooden tile in his pocket, Jake felt like a fake. *Jake-the-Fake.*

But at that moment, he recalled his grandpa's words: "It's not about being the best, Jax. It's about giving it your best." And that's when it hit him. *My grandpa didn't finish his quest. He didn't figure it all out. He had to pass it on to me.* Never once had Jake thought his grandpa had failed. He'd given his best with the time he'd been given. This truth filled Jake with a surge of hope. He looked around at the awesome landscape surrounding him, then focused his eyes on the dark crack in the canyon wall. His purpose was clear. His destination was set. He hiked faster.

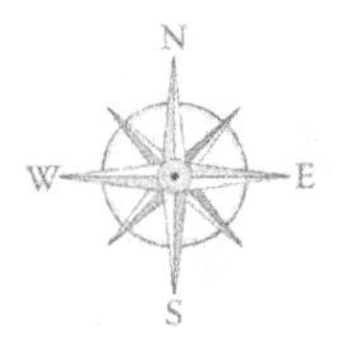

The faint trail Amber was following faded into a gravel-strewn wash. But she could still see the great rock that had pulled away from the canyon wall. With eyes fixed on her destination, she scrambled up a steep incline of loose gravel, sending rocks skittering from underneath her boots. She soon passed into the shadow of the massive chunk of stone. From a distance, it had appeared to be the size of a car. Up close, the rock was actually as big as a small house. Rounding the back corner, she stared up at a steep rock slab. It was only twenty feet to the top, but nervousness coursed through Amber's body. Ignoring it, she latched onto the rock face and climbed.

Cresting the top, she saw Agate, ten yards away. She was kneeling on the ground, clipping climbing equipment onto the gear loops of her harness. Amber ran to her and gave her a hug. "I'm so glad you're safe."

"Me, too," Agate replied. The metal climbing gear clinked as she moved. "I didn't see the second agent get into the raft. What happened?"

"It's a long story," Amber replied, "but what you need to know is that he followed us here to Havasupai Gardens."

Agate surveyed the landscape below them, her eyes scanning the thin, brown ribbon of the distant Bright Angel Trail.

“We’ve got a plan,” Amber continued. “Right now, Jake is luring him away from us.”

“Well-played, young padawan,” Agate said, throwing her a climbing harness. “Put this on. We’ve got a clue to find.”

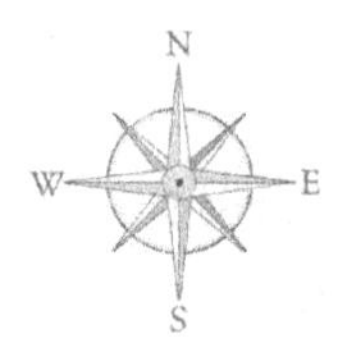

From behind him, Jake heard what sounded like a short burst of radio static. He stopped in his tracks but resisted the urge to turn around. Pressing on, he heard muted voices, then more static. The lightning bolt crevice loomed before him. Though not as big as the one in Rocky Mountain National Park, what had first looked like a thin cleft in the rock turned out to be big enough for him to squeeze inside.

Jake powered up the scree slope beneath the jagged fissure, his feet sliding backward one step with every two or three he took. The final segment was a steep band of exposed rock. He scrambled up it and crested the top of the incline. He now stood on the flat and broad shelf of rock that lined the base of the canyon wall. Chancing a glance behind him, all he could see was the green desert scrub and gray rock that fell away into the wash below. Without a doubt, the agent was hiding down there in the wash and watching. Jake turned and stared up at the sawtooth fracture in the cliff. At the top, it was just a thin line. But it grew wider as it tore its way to the opening that was now before him. He took in a deep breath and stepped into the darkness of the crack.

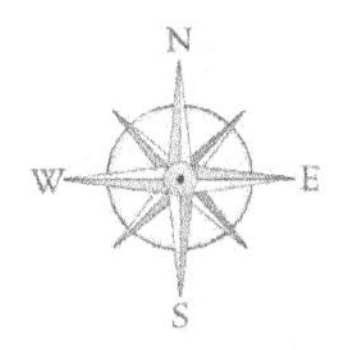

Inside the agent's tent, Wes half-zipped the door to keep himself hidden from view. Finding the agent's bag, he opened the largest compartment. It was empty. He tried a second pocket and then a third. "Oh my gosh, this pack has so many pockets," he muttered.

He gently felt the contours of the pack until he located the hard square edges of what felt like the cube. Gripping another zipper, he opened the compartment and pulled out a brown paper bag. The word *evidence* was printed on the outside in big, black letters. At the bottom of the bag, he read, *Property of the Federal Bureau of Investigation.* Wes paused. If the agents were fakes, why did they have real FBI stuff? He dumped the cube out of the evidence bag and slid it into his pocket. His heart beat faster. He might be stealing from a real FBI agent. *I sure hope I don't go to jail for this.*

He found and opened a second brown evidence bag and dumped the wooden tile into the palm of his hand. "Got it!"

Then, he heard footsteps on the gravel outside the tent.

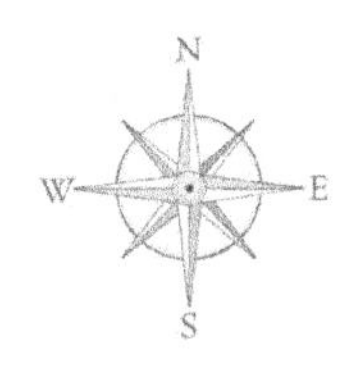

Jake crammed himself as far back into the crevice as he could go. The only sounds he could hear were his own breathing and the slosh of water in his hydration pack. He waited, taking deep breaths through his nose and letting them out slowly through his mouth. In the pale light, he watched his chest rise and fall and felt the deep throb of his quickened heartbeat as it pumped blood through the artery in his neck. A swift shadow passed across the fissure, followed by silence. Jake pulled the fake tile out of his pocket, took a final deep breath, and pressed himself back out into the blinding light.

Before his eyes could adjust to the intense light of the sun, a gruff voice called out, "Okay, kid, hand it over."

"Hand over what?" Jake played dumb.

"You know what—that little wooden scrap you found in there," the agent said, reaching out his massive hand."

Jake let his shoulders fall, then stretched out his hand and dropped the wooden tile into the man's open palm. His fingers wrapped around the object as he grinned at Jake.

"Kid, you're about as stupid as your grandfather."

A fire stirred in Jake's belly, and his hand instantly tightened into a fist.

"What did you say?" Jake demanded.

"I said that he was *stupid*."

Jake took a step toward the man, and his jaw locked. He could feel the pressure of his teeth pressing against one another.

"Your grandfather thought that he could take them down, beat them at their own game. But you can't win against men like them, Jake Evans. They're too powerful to be toppled." He made a sweeping gesture with his hands. "And they've got more money than they know what to do with."

"Then why are they after some old piece of wood?" Jake pointed to the man's hand that held the tile.

The agent laughed. "It's simple. Control. They believe they're better and know better than people like you and me."

"You're not like *me*," Jake spat.

"Oh, I know that, kid. I was once a true-blue like you—before they got to me. What I mean is you and me, and folks like your grandpa; we're just fleas on a dog to these people. And when they find it, they will have complete and endless control."

"What is *it*?" Jake asked. "What are they after?"

The man laughed again. "Kid, none of us know. Maybe your grandpa did. But I've got no idea. I'm paid handsomely to stay ignorant."

Jake still wanted to attack the massive man, but he found his feet frozen to the ground.

Then, a voice cut through the air, and Jake's eyes shot to the agent's belt. The man grabbed the radio and said, "Arcana here. Do you copy?"

"Loud and clear," the voice replied. "I have her location."

The agent pulled out what looked like a GPS unit and held it in his other hand. "Proceed with the coordinates."

"Thirty-six point zero..." the voice began. The agent punched the numbers into the device. "Negative one hundred twelve point one..."

The agent read back the numbers into the radio and waited.

"Affirmative. Over and out."

The agent switched off his radio and fastened it back on his belt. Holding the GPS, he scanned the canyon, turning to face northeast. Still staring at the GPS screen, he said, "Well, kid, it looks like I'm leaving with what I came for." He slipped the tile into his pocket. "Including the girl."

Jake's eyes locked on the eastern walls of Garden Creek Canyon, where Amber had gone to meet Agate.

"Your little escape plan yesterday worked—for a while, at least. But a couple of miles downriver, my partner caught on. Now he's sitting on a ridge"—he pointed to the north —"with an eighty-five-millimeter spotting scope. Seems that two climbers, one matching Agatha Albright's description, are roped up and attempting to ascend the east wall of Garden Creek Canyon."

Chapter 31

The Chase

Agate unbundled the rope and tied into her harness while Amber fed the other end through a belay device. After giving the rope a strong tug, Agate double-checked her harness knot. "You know how to belay

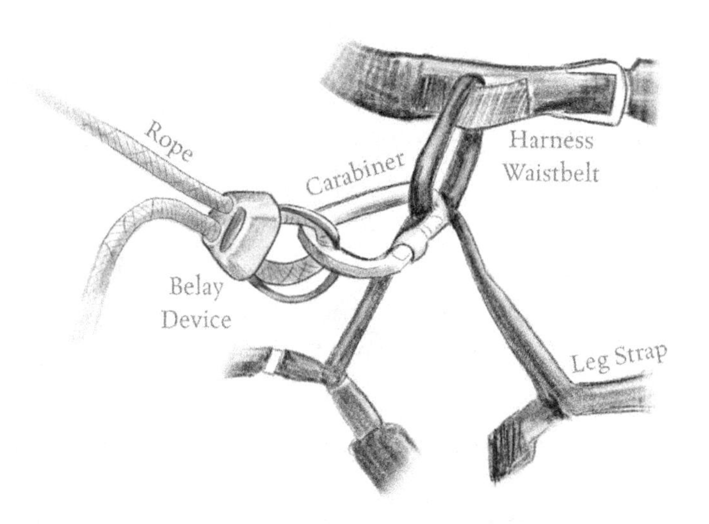

Amber nodded. "I belay for my dad, and he's almost twice as big as you."

Agate smiled and stepped up to Amber. They stood nose to nose. "We're almost the same size, which is about perfect. Still, if I take a fall from up there"—she pointed up the side of the canyon wall—"it's going to pull you right off the ground. As long as you're ready for it, you'll be fine."

"I'm good to go," Amber said.

Agate took a step back and surveyed the wall. "On belay?"

"Belay on," Amber called back.

"Climbing!" Agate called out

"Climb on." Agate gripped the rock and began her climb. *She is fast!* Amber began furiously taking in rope.

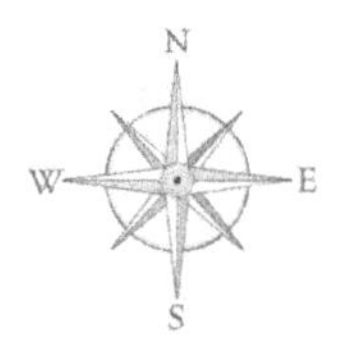

Wes held his breath and listened to the sounds outside the tent.

"Where did he go?" It was the voice of an older man.

"Maybe he went for a morning walk," the voice of a woman replied. "I bet he'll be back soon."

It was the older couple. Darn. Wes pounded his fist against his thigh.

"Let's come back in a few minutes," the woman suggested.

Wes cupped his hand behind his ear and listened as their

footsteps receded into the distance. He waited for what felt like forever. Then, he burst out of the tent and went immediately to the restroom building. He tried the first door, but it was occupied. He glanced at the cube in his hand, attempting to hide it against his body. The second door was also latched, and the third. He reached for the fourth door just as it swung open.

"Sorry, young man." It was the older woman. Wes dodged around her, slipped inside, and locked the door.

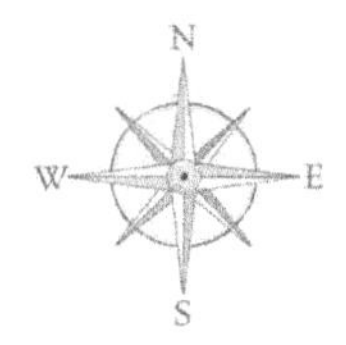

Jake bolted past the agent, scrambled down the rocky incline, and hurled himself down into the gulch. The man was definitely bigger and stronger, but Jake was certain he could beat the man in a footrace. The steep and rocky terrain flew by as he jumped over cacti, scrambled over boulders, and tore through gravel washes that led back toward the campground. Stealing a glance over his shoulder, he found the man struggling but still going faster than Jake had thought possible. Without stopping, he guzzled water through the tube attached to his daypack. At the bottom of the wash, his progress was slowed by the undergrowth and scrub trees. Jake crashed through a thicket of brush and was surprised to find himself on the hard packed earth of the Bright Angel Trail.

Sprinting down the dirt trail, Jake caught sight of the landmark Amber had described yesterday. It looked like a giant's hand had wrenched the rock from the canyon wall. Above the rock and to his left, he could make out two human figures barely visible against the mottled red rock, Amber and Agate. With his throat on fire, he found the hidden trail. His feet pounded through the wash and into the steep gulch.

His lungs burned with every breath, but he forced himself to keep running. Each stride drained him of energy. His sprint slowed to a stumbling jog. Halting to catch his breath, he saw the agent, still far off but racing down Bright Angel Trail. Jake had to keep going.

His adrenaline surged, and he pushed himself harder. He could clearly see Agate now. She had climbed to a narrow ledge, still a hundred feet below the ancient granaries. He was soaked in sweat, and his breath came in short bursts as he scrambled up the loose stones to the base of the massive fractured rock.

Beads of sweat dripped down Jake's forehead as he stared at the imposing rock slab. He could see the top. It was only twenty feet away, but his aching legs felt like concrete. Could he make it? He had no choice. The agent was coming and fast. Jake gripped the rock, then found a foothold. Pulling himself up, he found another hold. Inch by inch, he clawed his way up. His hands shook. His grip faltered.

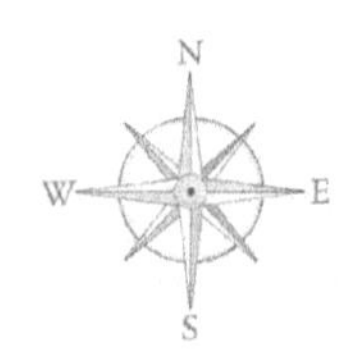

Amber watched Agate pull herself onto a narrow ledge and then saw her smile vanish, replaced by furrows of concern across her brow. Agate stared at something behind and below Amber. Amber turned and heard what sounded like Jake's voice call out, "Help. I need help!"

"It's Jake!" Agate called down. "He's climbing up the wall behind you. I'm safe here. Unclip and help him."

Amber hesitated. She knew that you never unclip when your partner is climbing. She looked back up. "Go, now!" Agate yelled.

Amber unclipped her belay device and ran to the lip of the wall that Jake was attempting to climb. But she couldn't reach him. She lay down on her belly and strained to press her fingers toward him.

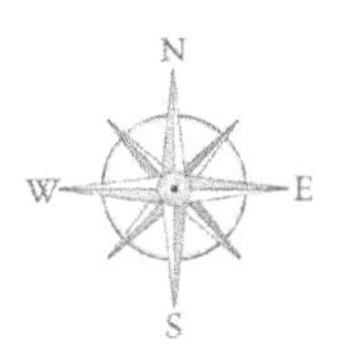

Jake stretched as far as he could, his right foot nearly slipping from the smooth rock beneath it.

"You're going to have to make one more move," Amber said. "Search with your toes to find a foothold."

Jake bent his knee, pulling his leg up, and blindly probed the rock with the toe of his boot.

"Oh, no," Amber gasped. "The agent. He's coming."

"I know," Jake grunted, desperately trying to find something his foot could catch. Then he found it. It wasn't much, but it was enough. Pressing as hard as he could with his right leg, he shot his hand out to Amber. She grabbed his wrist, and his fingers clasped around hers. He continued to climb with his legs and free hand. Amber pulled, and he climbed with all his strength. Cresting the lip of the rock wall, he collapsed in the red dirt.

"Guys!" Agate called down. "That rock wall will slow him down"—she pointed below to where the agent approached the rock—"but not long enough. We've got to change up our plan. Amber, clip back in. I'm coming down."

Agate rappelled down the canyon wall, then unfastened and slipped out of her harness. She handed it to Amber. "You're going to have to make the climb." She grabbed Jake's shoulder and looked him in the eye. "And you're going to have to belay."

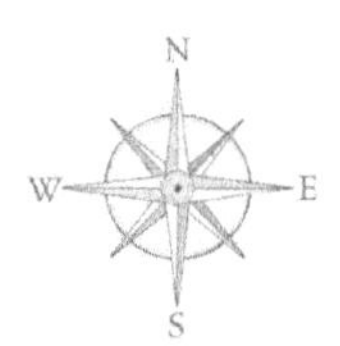

Wes unlatched the restroom door, and it slowly swung open. Taking a deep breath, he plunged ahead, back toward camp.

"Stop!" demanded a voice from behind him. "Give it to us. Now."

Wes spun around to see the older couple standing five paces away.

"I don't know what you're talking about," Wes replied.

"Open your pack," the woman commanded.

Wes slowly unshouldered his daypack and unzipped it. The woman marched up, thrust her hand into the compartment, and clutched hold of the wooden object. She then walked back to her husband and handed it to him.

"Kid, didn't your parents teach you not to steal?" the man mocked.

Wes hung his head, dejected.

Then the man dropped the cube onto the ground, lifted his boot, and with a single blow, crushed it into the dirt.

They stared at Wes while grinding what was left of the object into splinters. Wes looked down at the crushed cube lying beside the man's boot. His mouth hung open. Then he said through gritted teeth, "You two are like the meanest old people I've ever met."

He glanced down at the cube again. "I mean...I mean..."

"You mean what?" the man asked.

"I mean that if you were my grandparents, I'd disown you. I'd file for grandparent-divorce."

"I don't think that's possible, kid."

"I'm just saying that if it was, *I would*!" Wes balled his hands into fists while his face grew almost as red as his hair. He shook his head in disbelief. "Plus, you've destroyed the map. The Director is going to be furious with you two."

The woman pulled a piece of paper from her pocket. "We have all we need right here." She winked. Wes could see it was a drawing of the cube map, just like the one he'd been working on.

"We drew in the third piece, and our friend over there"—she gestured toward the agent's tent— "will soon have the fourth one. The Director didn't care about that little box."

She kicked aside the pieces of the broken cube. "He only wants the map."

Wes continued glaring at the couple. Then he turned away and slumped his shoulders. After trudging back to camp, he entered the tent and zipped himself inside.

Agate looked at Jake. "Amber filled me in on the plan. Did it work?"

"Yeah, he stole the fake tile from me," Jake answered.

"Good," she said, grabbing her bug-out bag and throwing it over her shoulder. "If he believes he has the fourth clue, then all he cares about now is capturing me." She looked them each in the eyes. "I'm the decoy now, okay. Don't worry about me. Get the clue. And keep it safe."

"We can't let you get captured," Jake replied.

"I've got a backup plan. I scoped it out last night. There's a chimney in the rock, just around the corner. It's an easy climb to the plateau above us. Once I'm a hundred yards into it, the agent won't be able to follow. He's too big. From there, I can make my way to Yavapai Point. I'll have radio reception there and can lay low on the rim."

"What if you fall?" Amber asked.

"I won't. I promise. But keep the radio. Tomorrow, when you're back on the rim, I'll make contact to let you know that I'm safe and sound."

Jake didn't like this. He knew Agate was a competitive climber, but this was not a good scenario. Alone. In the Grand Canyon. And climbing. It was a recipe for disaster. But he couldn't think of any better option.

"Water," he said. "Agate, take my water. You'll need it." He pulled the hydration bag out of his pack and handed it to her.

Agate clipped it to the side of her pack with a carabiner. "Okay," she said. "You two, hide behind that boulder. When the agent climbs up, I'll give him just enough time to see me before I bolt. Eventually, he'll give up and leave. Wait until he climbs back down and is out of sight. Then, climb." She handed Amber her helmet.

Jake and Amber crept behind the boulder. It was cool in the shadowed space. Jake could peer around its side without being seen. He could hear the agent approaching, his heavy breathing, and the sound of his boots scraping against the rock. A hand appeared, then another, and the agent pulled himself onto the shelf. Seeing Agate, he shot to his feet.

Agate shot across the stone ledge. They both rounded a corner in the canyon wall and disappeared.

The world was still and silent. "I'll be back," Jake whispered. He crawled out from behind the boulder and began creeping along the red rock wall. He flattened himself against the rock and listened. Nothing. He crept forward and rounded the bulge in the canyon wall and could now hear the sounds of struggle.

Peering around the rock, he could see the long, narrow chimney. Small boulders and rocks had, over hundreds of years, spilled into and choked the slot in the canyon wall. Agate had wedged herself into the confined space and was frantically trying to put distance between her and her pursuer. The agent shot out his hand and caught the waist belt of her backpack. Agate kicked with fury, trying to cling to the rock and free herself from his grip. Gritty rubble skipped off the walls of the crag, skittering to the ground at Jake's feet.

Jake didn't hesitate. He burst from his hiding place behind the wall. He scrambled into the crag, latched onto the man's boot, and yanked as hard as he could. At that same moment, Agate's foot found the man's nose. The agent pitched backward, tumbling over Jake and knocking him from the rock. Jake sailed through the air and landed with a dull thud on the agent's ribcage. They tumbled down a steep gravel wash until they came to a stop.

Jake blinked and opened his eyes. After clearing the dust from his eyelashes, he stood up. "Jake!" He turned to see Agate, who had climbed back down from the crag.

He was amazed. Other than a few scratches, he was fine. "I'm okay."

"He doesn't look so good," she pointed to the agent, who was now on his back, holding his side and groaning. "You help him. I'm going to belay Amber."

Jake watched Agate vanish around the jutting canyon wall. Jake turned back and slowly approached the man. He was covered in dust and scrapes, and his breathing was labored.

He kneeled beside the man and attempted to cast a

shadow across the agent's face. A small kindness for someone who had been so mean. "Are you bleeding anywhere?" Jake asked.

The agent shook his head. "I'm okay, kid." With a grunt, he attempted to get to his feet, but his ankle gave way, and he collapsed back onto the ground. Shutting his eyes, he let out a long sigh of defeat.

"Mister," Jake said.

"Yeah," the man breathed.

"Promise me that you'll leave Agate alone," Jake said.

"Are you making demands now, kid?" The man propped himself up on his elbow and winced.

"I guess so," Jake answered. "Promise me."

"I promise," he replied. "But the Director won't stop. He'll send others."

"And I want you to take back what you said," Jake stood, casting a long shadow across the man.

"Take back what?" the man said, scrunching his eyes.

"My grandpa. You called him stupid," Jake said. "Take it back."

"I take it back, kid. I'm sorry. All I meant is that you can't fight these guys and win. I tried and gave up. They always win."

"You fought them?" Jake asked in surprise.

"Like I said, I tried. You can't imagine how powerful they are, kid."

"Well, give the Director a message from me then. Tell him, or her, or whoever they are, that I won't stop," Jake said. "My grandpa didn't stop, and neither will I."

"Okay, kid, whatever." The agent coughed and winced. "I'll tell the Director."

"I'm going to check on my friends, and then I'll get you some help."

As Jake turned to leave, a thought hit him, and a smile lit across his face. He turned back to the agent. "One more thing."

"What's that?"

"I want your jacket."

Chapter 32

The Climb

Amber stretched her arm as high as she could and clipped into one of the anchors Agate had set into the rock. After several moves and clipping into two more anchors, Amber reached the narrow ledge and pulled herself up. She could see all the way out to Havasupai Gardens, down to Agate below her, and Jake, who was still beside the agent, shielding his eyes from the sun and watching her. He gave her a thumbs up. She smiled and returned the sign.

"There are a lot of good holds on your left, but follow the crack," Agate called up. "Set one of the big cams in just above your head."

Amber nodded, unfastened a cam device from the gear loop of her harness, and slid the cam into the crack. After yanking hard to test it, she slipped the rope through the carabiner at the near end of the device. She looked down to

Agate, who kept her hands on the ropes and nodded her approval. Using the crack and the holds on her left, Amber continued her climb.

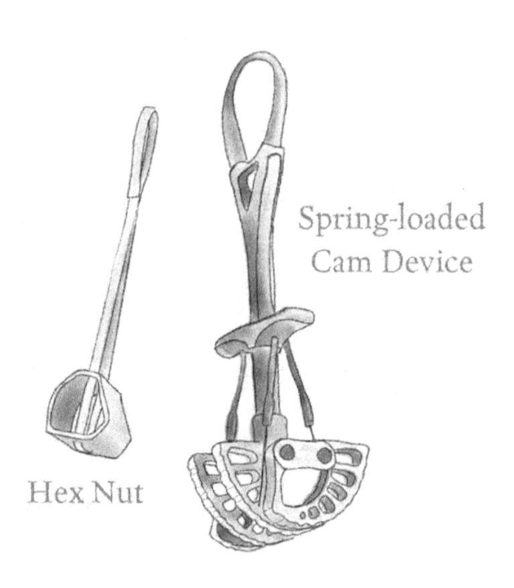

"If the crack is narrow, you can use a hex," Agate called up. "Otherwise, keep using the cams. You've got plenty."

Holding on to the rock with her left hand, Amber wedged a hex stopper into the crack, slipped the rope through its carabiner, and looked for her next move. With every move up the wall, she could feel Agate take in the slack, and the rope tighten. She continued the process: climb, place a cam or hex, clip in, and climb again until she reached the slanted lip of the granary ledge. She hooked her heel onto the lip and pulled as hard as she could to bring her body over the top. What she saw next took her breath away.

Four mud and rock structures lined a low overhang. Amber looked closer and could see fingerprints left by the builders in the hardened mud. Peeking through the low doorway of the nearest granary, she saw shards of pottery and corn cobs, left over a thousand years ago by the Ancestral Puebloans who had made the canyon their home. It felt weird, like she was intruding upon someone's home. During her climb, she'd wondered how anyone could possibly manage the ascent without ropes and gear. But examining the wall above the granary, she found the answer: a series of hand and footholds had been carved into the rock face. Because the wall above her slanted toward the upper rim, someone could climb down to the granaries, likely with heavy baskets of corn on their backs. Even with the holds, it would have been a dizzying and daunting task.

Agate's voice called up to her. Amber approached the edge, looked down, and put her hand behind her ear so she could hear.

"It's red!" Agate called out. "The clue is red."

Amber turned and spotted it almost immediately. Tucked between the ceiling of the overhang and the ancient stonework was a rust-covered, red object. Carefully, she gave it a tug and pried the metal thing loose from the rock. As she did, something rattled inside.

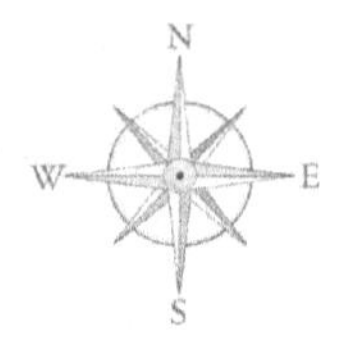

Jake stared up at the granaries as Amber came to the edge holding an object in her hand.

"I found it!" Her voice echoed off the canyon walls.

Jake jumped up and down and pumped his fist.

"Hey, kid, are you going to get me some help or what?"

"Oh, yeah, sure thing," he replied. In his excitement, Jake had nearly forgotten about the agent.

"Amber!" Agate called up. "Stay right there. I need to talk with Jake."

She motioned to Jake, and he ran to a spot where he'd be close enough to hear her.

"After Amber is down, I'm bugging out," she called down. "Before I go, I wanted to say thanks for helping me." He could see her smile. "You're a good friend, Jake Evans."

Jake's heart filled with a mix of relief and happiness. *A good friend.* He hoped Amber would say the same thing.

"Okay, go get that guy some help."

With that, Jake took off, sprinting back to Havasupai Gardens.

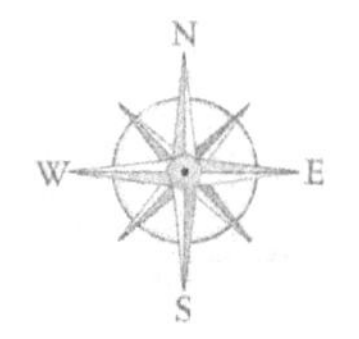

After Jake alerted the ranger, he ran back to help Amber. She and Agate had already packed up the climbing gear, and Agate was gone. He had brought a water bottle with him for the agent. He nodded at Jake when he handed it to him. "Thanks, kid. And I'll remember. I promise."

Back at camp, their families had gathered for breakfast. Wes was already at the picnic table. He looked up from his bowl, "It's oatmeal, but pretty good." He had picked out all the raisins and set them on a napkin.

"Did you get it?"

Amber held the old metal tin out in her hand and gave it a shake. Wes's eyebrows rose almost to the top of his forehead. "What's in it?"

"We don't know yet," Jake replied. "We wanted to wait and open it together."

Amber gave Wes a serious look. "Did you get the cube? And the tile?"

Wes bit his lip and nodded.

"Hey, kids," Uncle Brian called out. "We need to be packed up and out of here in *one hour*."

"Okay, Dad," Wes said as he unfastened the band of his watch. "I'm taking this off now"—he held the watch up in the air for his dad to see—"and I'm going to sit on it."

Uncle Brian's eyebrows knit with confusion. "Why would you do that?"

Wes grinned, "Because I want to be *on time*."

Uncle Brian, Jake, and Amber all shook their heads.

"It's your fault, Uncle Brian," Jake said. "Bad jokes are in your genetic code, and you passed them on to Wes."

"I take full responsibility." Uncle Brian walked over and gave Wes a squeeze.

"You walked right into that one, Dad," Wes replied.

"I did. That reminds me, what time do ducks wake up in the morning?" Uncle Brian paused. The three kids stared at him, ready to cringe at the answer. "At the quack of dawn."

Wes punched his dad in the side. "That was terrible. You can do better than that."

"I know. But I had really hoped that one would *quack* you up."

All three kids groaned as Uncle Brian walked away.

Jake grabbed his bowl of oatmeal and stood up. "Let's go to our campsite and talk."

Moments later, Amber and Jake sat down at the picnic table across from Wes. "Okay, Wes, you go first," Jake said.

"Well, remember those old people?" Wes glared at Jake and Amber.

"Yeah," Amber replied. "The ones you think are bad guys?"

"The ones who *are* bad guys." Wes took the last bite of his breakfast and pushed the bowl aside. "Guess who showed up when I was in the agent's tent?"

"That couple?" Jake asked.

"I told you guys they were bad news. And it gets worse. I found the cube and the tile, but I had to wait for them to leave. When they finally left, I slipped out of the tent and ran over to the restroom." Wes paused. "And when I came out, they were waiting."

"What did they want?" Amber asked.

"The cube," Wes replied.

"What did you do?" Jake set his spoon down on the table.

"I gave it to them," Wes answered.

"You did what?" Jake pressed both his hands onto the table.

"And the old guy; he stomped it into the ground." Wes threw his hands in the air.

Jake could feel the blood drain out of his face.

"I didn't see that coming—the stomping the cube part," Wes said. "But I expected something like that would happen. Either that old couple or the agent might catch me, so I kinda made a backup plan without telling you guys."

Jake and Amber were in shock, intently listening to Wes.

"So, you know how I made the fake tile out of that old wood yesterday?"

Jake and Amber nodded.

"Well, I also made a fake cube," Wes explained.

"A fake cube?" Jake whispered back to his cousin.

"Yeah. It was pretty simple. I found nails in some of the wood, and I borrowed a hammer from that shed behind the canteen."

"So, the old guy crushed a fake cube?" Amber asked. "Not the real one?"

"Exactly!" Wes replied, slamming his fists onto the table in excitement.

Amber half collapsed onto the table, and Jake held his head in his hands.

"You scared us to death!" Jake said. "I feel like reaching across and shaking you."

"Sorry." Wes paused, then smiled. "Well, I guess that I'm not sorry. You two didn't believe me about that old couple. You need to start trusting my intuition."

"I still feel like I'm going to be sick," Jake replied. "Okay, I'm sorry for not trusting you." Jake squinted at Wes. "So, where's the real cube and the clue?"

"Come with me," he said. "I wanted to finish my breakfast before doing this. You probably should, too."

"Why?" Amber asked.

Wes shot her a serious grin. "This is definitely one of those times when you should trust my intuition."

They followed Wes, who led them to the restroom building, where he opened one of the doors and walked inside. After the door swung closed, they heard Wes gag and cough. They looked at each other with confused expressions. A moment later, Wes returned with a large Ziploc bag lined with duct tape across the top. They could clearly see the cube and the clue inside.

"I hid it where no one would look," Wes explained. "Inside the top of the pit toilet."

"Oh my gosh," Amber said, cringing. She turned her head away from Wes. "I think I *am* going to be sick."

Jake took a step back from the bag. "You've got to be kidding me, Wes. Nobody in their right mind would do that."

"Exactly! That's why I hid it there. And I almost lost my breakfast getting it out."

"That's so gross." Amber scrunched up her face. "And... so brilliant."

"Why, thank you," Wes replied, obviously very pleased with himself. "Okay, now we should open that old metal thing and get the final clue."

"Um, could you maybe, first go wash your hands?" Jake asked.

"On it!" Wes ran to the hand sanitizer dispenser attached to the outside of the restroom.

When he returned, Amber pulled the metal tin out of her backpack and handed it to Jake.

"No, you found it," Jake said. "You get to open it."

They all read the front of the rusted red container: *Prince Albert Crimp Cut Long Burning Tobacco.*

"It's an old tobacco case," Wes whispered. "It would be super disappointing if Amber opened it and dumped out a bunch of ancient tobacco."

The top pinched and creaked as Amber pried it open. She emptied the contents into her hand. It was unmistakable. The fourth wooden tile lay in her palm, the piece they needed to complete the map. But there was something else along with it, a small folded piece of paper that looked as old as the tobacco container itself. Amber handed the wooden tile to Jake, the tin to Wes, and then gently unfolded the note. It read: *1.5, 3, IG, PC. 5 and 6 are in IG. 5=NE. 6=SW.*

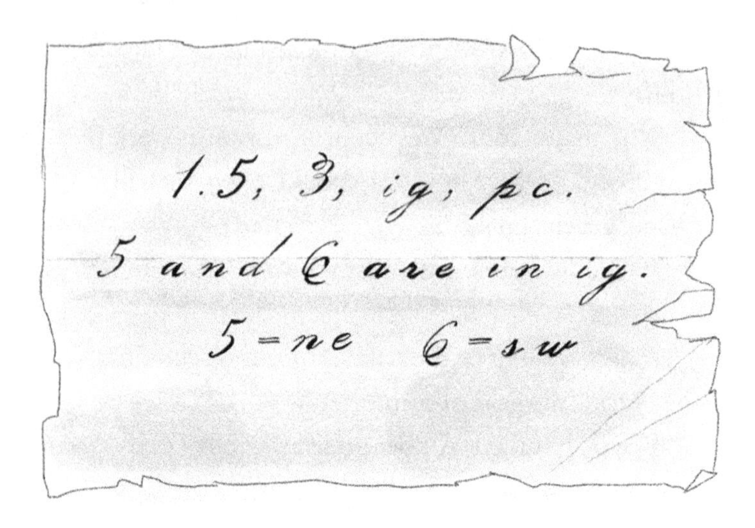

1.5, 3, ig, pc.

5 and 6 are in ig.

5=ne 6=sw

Wes's forehead wrinkled. “What! There are two *more* clues?”

Chapter 33

Five and Six

Amber pulled her phone out of her back pocket and took a picture of the note. She handed it to Jake. "Be careful. It's super brittle."

Jake held the note in his palm, and Wes moved beside him to get a better look.

"Oh, no." Amber looked at the time on her phone. "We've only got thirty minutes before we have to leave."

"And we're not even packed," Wes replied.

The kids ran to their campsite and sat down to ponder the note. Jake unfolded the topographic map of the Grand Canyon and set it on the table.

"The *SW* and *NE* parts are easy," Wes said. "Those have to be southwest and northeast."

"And *IG* could mean Indian Garden," Amber offered. "That's what it would have been called back when the note was written."

"Yeah," Jake said, setting his finger on Indian Garden.

"This map was printed before the name was changed to Havasupai." Jake traced the Bright Angel Trail. "Guys, look at this! There's a resthouse near the top called *1.5 Mile Resthouse.*"

"And the next one is *3 Mile Resthouse,*" Wes set his finger beside the shelter symbol on the map.

"That matches," Amber said, setting the note on top of the map. "Are there more resthouses?"

Jake scanned the dashed line of the trail and set his finger near the base of the Bright Angel Trail, near the Colorado River. "Just this one, the River Resthouse. But it doesn't match the note. Wouldn't there be an *R* or *RR*?"

"Wait, that's where we stopped yesterday," Wes said. "Remember when I signed that hiker log?"

"Yes!" Jake clapped his hands. "That logbook had a different name on it, *Pipe something.*"

"Pipe Creek!" Wes said, pointing to a spot on the map. "That makes sense. It's right where Pipe Creek meets the Colorado River."

Amber picked up the note. "That matches. *PC* probably means Pipe Creek."

"Can I see that?" Jake asked.

Amber handed him the note, and he read it out loud: "*1.5, 3, IG, PC. 5 and 6 are in IG. 5=NE. 6=SW.*"

"So, if *IG* means Indian Garden, then there must be an old shelter house right here," Jake said, pointing to the ground at their feet.

The kids locked eyes with one another. Jake knew they were all thinking the exact same thought.

They bolted out of their seats and ran down a side path. Finding the stone steps, they descended into the shelter house where they had made their plans the day before. Wes, still breathing heavily, pulled out his compass. Holding it out in front of him, he turned his body until he was facing southwest. "So, the last clue should be...somewhere here along the back wall," he said. Wes quickly turned around. "And the fifth clue should be somewhere here." He pointed out the front entrance of the resthouse.

They scanned the front and back walls, tugged on the stones, tapped for loose mortar, but everything was held tightly in place. Then Jake's eyes fell upon the open rafters. "Holy cow!"

Amber and Wes spun around as Jake pointed toward the ceiling. "There it is!"

Supporting the rafters, a thick beam rested on the stone corner pillars of the shelter. Between that beam and the rafter beam, was a cube of wood, its face a perfect square. And into the square, someone had carved a symbol.

"You've got to be kidding me!" Wes said, palming his face. "We were sitting right here yesterday and had no idea!"

"To be fair," Amber replied, "we also had no idea there were *two* more clues."

Jake turned around to face the back of the shelter and found the same cube of wood supporting the rafters and another carving on its surface.

Amber zoomed in on the cubes and shot pictures of both. "Hey, boys, come over here. Let's get a pic of us." With Jake and Wes on either side, Amber shot a selfie of them with one of the rafter clues in the background.

"We need a team name." A wide grin lit upon Wes's face. "How about *The Triple Threat*."

Jake and Amber looked at the ground and shook their heads.

"What? I thought it was really good."

"Sorry, Wes, I think we're good without a team name," Jake said.

"Well, can't blame me for trying," Wes replied.

At that moment, Amber's dad appeared in the entryway, his backpack slung over his shoulders. "Aren't you three ready? We're about to head out."

"Sorry, Dad," Amber called back. "We've got to pack."

Mr. Catalina shook his head as the kids booked it back to the campsite. The boys quickly tore down their tent and crammed their gear into the backpacks. Amber returned in less than five minutes. "My mom packed our tent already," she explained. The kids ran to the water spigot and began filling their hydration bags. Jake filled his water bottle, and one he'd borrowed from his cousin. The parents, all ready to depart, were gathered alongside the trail, laughing about something, when a team of rangers came by supporting the limping FBI agent.

Everyone fell silent as he passed. Jake heard his mom ask, "Wonder what happened to him?"

Jake looked at his friends and winked.

Chapter 34

Leaving

Amber held the map as they hiked up the Bright Angel Trail. "It's four and a half miles to the top, and *three thousand* feet of elevation gain."

Wes slumped and began hiking with his arms hanging at his sides swaying back and forth.

"What are you doing?" Jake asked.

"My sad elephant walk. You should try it. It helps you feel all the disappointment."

"Why would I want to feel disappointed?"

"Because feelings are like waves," Wes replied. "At least that's what my mom says. And if you feel them all the way through, they don't get stuck. Seriously, try it out. Think about how tough this hike is going to be and do the sad elephant."

Jake and Amber both slouched over, swaying their arms as they walked. After a few seconds, Jake stood up straight again.

"You've got to do it for at least a full minute for it to work," Wes urged. "You've got to *feel* the whole thing in your *whole* body."

Jake laughed at the sight of Amber and Wes but joined them again just for the fun of it.

"You're right," Amber said. "It really does work."

"It sure beats listening to you guys whining about how hard this hike is," Wes replied.

"When do I ever whine?" Amber asked.

Wes straightened and began walking normally again. "Okay, that's fair. Pretty much never. It's more me and Jake who do all the whining."

Two hours later, they neared the end of the demanding journey, just below the South Rim.

"Check that out!" Jake called. He pointed up to a pictograph panel, where several deer with spiky antlers had been painted onto the overhang. The deep red paint made the figures leap out from the limestone.

Wes had stopped at an interpretive sign. "Those drawings are four thousand years old!"

"They remind me of the markings on the arrowhead drawing in the old journal we found in Rocky Mountain National Park," Amber added. She snapped a photo of the panel.

Jake stared up at the red animals. "And reminds me of the cube."

"Speaking of the cube," Wes said, "when are we going to put it all together?"

"As soon as we can sit down," Jake answered. "We should keep moving. The faster we hike, the sooner we can rest."

Amber looked over her shoulder. "My mom said we're getting burgers at the top."

Wes stopped in his tracks. "Did you say...*burgers*?"

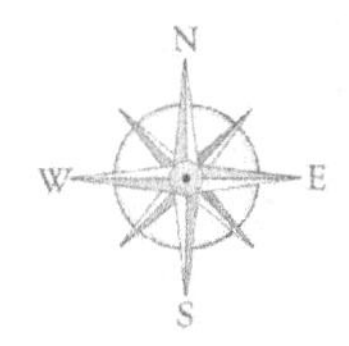

The last hundred yards of the trail were choked with hikers dressed in fresh clothes and slathered in sunscreen. The three friends labored through the last stretch, their boots covered in dust and shirts drenched in sweat.

Wes sniffed the air. "I forgot what shampoo and soap smelled like."

A family passed them, and one of the kids asked his parents, "Did they hike from all the way down there?" He pointed down into the canyon.

"We sure did," Jake replied. The parents and three other kids turned and looked at Jake, Amber, and Wes with wide eyes.

"Almost twenty miles to the Colorado River and back," Jake added.

"No way," the little boy replied.

"Well, we didn't do it all in one day," Jake explained. "And when you're our age, I bet you could do it too."

The boy's parents smiled.

Moments later, Jake's feet crested the top of the Bright Angel Trail. The kids now stood among an overwhelming crowd of visitors taking selfies, talking, and gasping at the views. After finding their parents, they walked to the burger place, and the kids sat down at their own table. Jake pulled the cube from his pack and laid it flat on the table.

Wes looked over both of his shoulders. "Don't you think it's risky to have that thing out in the open?"

"I think we're safe," Jake replied. "We kind of took care of the agents."

Wes nodded and smiled.

Using his grandpa's diagram, Jake set the first tile in its place. Amber took the drawing of the second tile and did the same. Wes pulled out the tile he'd recovered from the agent's tent and slid it into spot three. Jake handed the fourth tile to Amber. "You climbed for it." She set it in its place.

The final two tiles were still on Amber's phone. She pulled it out and turned it on.

"Make sure you turn off your cell connection," Wes said.

"You don't want the Director hacking your phone and getting those pictures."

Amber immediately switched the phone to airplane mode, found the photo, then set it on the table.

"I can draw them," Wes offered. Using a black crayon, he copied the photos of tiles five and six onto a napkin. "I can't believe they still give me a kid's menu and crayons," he huffed. "I'm almost thirteen."

Jake studied the napkin tiles. "My grandpa's drawing only had spaces for *four* tiles, so we've got to figure this out. Maybe we can line up the markings." Jake slid Wes's paper squares in place.

"What do you think?"

"Looks like a perfect fit," Amber said.

The three kids gazed at the completed map in wonder.

"Well, we've got a map," Wes said, "but to what?"

"It has to be to one of the parks we're going to visit," Amber said.

"If it is," Jake replied, "this thing was made hundreds of years before any of those parks existed."

Wes picked up one of the tiles and flipped it over. "No way! It says *Yellowstone* on the back."

Jake's and Amber's eyes grew wide. Wes slowly grinned. "Just kidding."

Amber huffed. "You're lucky I'm not sitting closer, or I'd punch you in the leg—and hard."

Wes laughed. "Sorry. I couldn't resist."

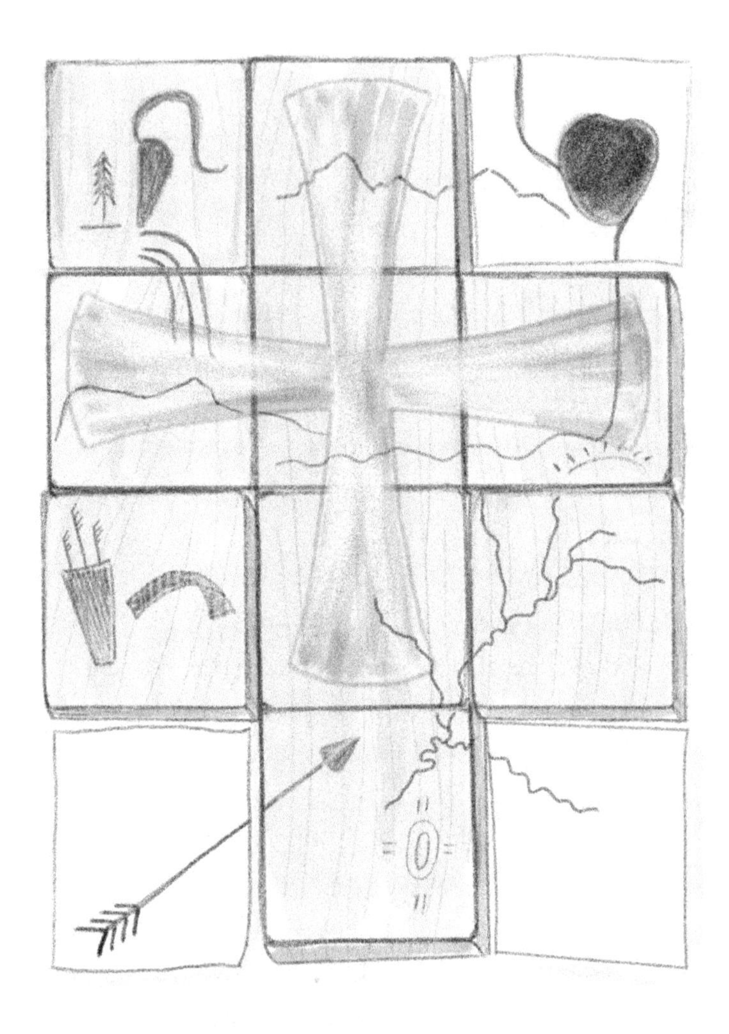

"We'll figure it out," Jake said. "Remember: *it all goes back to the scrapbook*. There's got to be something that will lead us to the right spot. Right now, we should celebrate."

The waitress arrived balancing a tray full of burgers and fries. "I've got a triple-bacon cheeseburger."

Wes's hand shot into the air. "That would be me."

The waitress set their plates on the table, and the kids dug in. "Agate said your grandpa found a bunch of treasures," Wes said between bites. "Not one. Not two. A *bunch of them.*"

At the mention of Agate's name, Amber looked at her watch and began fishing around in her backpack. "It's almost noon. I totally forgot. We need to check on Agate." She pulled out the radio.

Jake's head swirled with questions. He'd been so distracted by the events of the last two days that he'd almost forgotten. *Grandpa found Long Tom's treasure. And a bunch of others. Where did he hide them? Would the scavenger hunt lead them to some secret stash in one of the parks? And was Agate safe? Would they hear from her?*

Radio static interrupted his thoughts. "Agate, this is Amber; come in."

Nothing. Amber tried another radio channel. "Agate, do you read me?"

"Loud and clear." Agate's voice came from the other end. "Going to keep my twenty on the down-low in case we've got eavesdroppers. I'm safe and sound. Over and out."

Wes dropped his burger onto his plate. "Over and out? She didn't even let us talk to her."

"She's playing it safe," Jake explained.

Wes took another bite, covered his mouth and with his mouth full of food said, "Thut miks sinz."

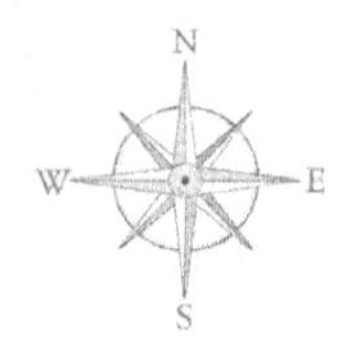

The next morning, everyone slept in. After breakfast, they packed up to leave. The three vehicles—the two trucks with campers in tow, and the RV—formed a caravan. They had a five-hour drive to their next stop, Zion National Park, and Jake had decided to get some time alone resting in the back seat of the truck. Before departing Mather Campground, Jake's mom pulled the truck up to the campground office to let the staff know they were checking out early. She returned with a package addressed to Jake. "Maybe it's more future mail from your grandpa?" But Jake noticed the postmark and the date: *Grand Canyon Village, June 11th*. It had been mailed that very morning.

"Mom, I think I've changed my mind," Jake said. "I'm going to ride in the RV with Wes and Amber."

"Okay," she replied. "But make sure you get some rest. You're looking pretty worn out."

"I promise." He jumped out of the truck with the package and ran back to the RV. Inside, he found Wes deep in thought, studying the drawing of the cube map, and Amber drawing in her sketchbook.

Wes looked up. "You riding with us now?"

Jake smiled. "Yeah." He plopped down beside Amber and hid the package on his lap. His friends were so engrossed in what they were doing, they didn't notice that he had brought something with him.

"Did you figure that map out yet?" Jake asked.

"Maybe," Wes answered. "At least this part of it." His eyes appeared mesmerized by the paper. "This looks like a river or a bunch of creeks." Wes set his finger on a series of markings, and then looked across the table to Jake.

"I got you something." Jake threw the package down on the table. "Hurry up and open it."

Wes gave his cousin a surprised look and set the paper aside. He tore into the package, and his surprise turned to complete shock. "What in the world...are you kidding? But, how did you?"

Jake smiled.

Wes pulled the FBI jacket out of the package and immediately put it on.

Epilogue

"Mom and Dad," Wes called up to the front of the RV.

"Yeah?" they both replied.

"Can we watch a movie?"

"Sure," his mom replied. "Just keep the sound at a reasonable level."

"Thanks," all three kids said in unison.

"Amber, why don't you pick this time?" Jake offered.

Wes got up and slid both hands into his pockets. He spun around to show off the jacket. Then he froze.

"Wes, you okay?" Jake asked.

Wes slowly turned to face his cousin. Then he drew his hand from the pocket of the FBI jacket. It held an envelope. Wes looked at the front and then handed it to Jake.

"It's addressed to you."

Author's Notes

Visiting Grand Canyon National Park

South Rim

Like Jake's family, most people visit the South Rim of the Grand Canyon. And fewer than 1% actually hike all the way down to the bottom. And that's for good reasons. First, the almost 8 to 10-mile hike to the bottom (depending on the trail you take) is incredibly demanding. Campground spaces are extremely limited, and the journey requires a lot of preparation. Second, there's a lot to see and do along the South Rim. I'll be building out a full Grand Canyon Visitors Guide at NationalParkMysterySeries.com, but for now, here are a few ideas if your family plans to visit:

- Mather Point: Take in the views Jake and his friends enjoyed at this iconic outlook. Get up early and catch the sunrise when fewer people are there.

- Desert View Watchtower: This seven-story stone tower was designed by Mary Colter, the same architect who planned the cabins and canteen at Phantom Ranch.
- Hike the Bright Angel Trail: From the trailhead, you can hike down to 1) 1.5 Mile Resthouse, 2) 3 Mile Resthouse, or 3) Havasupai Gardens (4.5 miles one way/9 miles round trip).
- Hike the South Kaibab Trail: From the trailhead, it's 1 mile to Ooh Ahh Point or 1.5 miles to Cedar Ridge.
- Train Ride: Take a train through pine forest and desert landscapes from Williams to the South Rim. Visit https://www.thetrain.com for details.
- Mule Trips: There are two-hour rides and overnight trips down to Phantom Ranch. For more information, visit https://www.grand-canyonlodges.com/plan/mule-rides/

North Rim

The North Rim area is more remote, so it receives fewer visitors.

- Take the short hike out to Bright Angel Point for amazing views.
- Take a scenic drive along the Cape Royal Road, and hike out 1 mile one-way to Cape Royal. Be sure to take the side trail to view Angels Window.

- Mule Rides: https://www.canyon-rides.com/grand-canyon-mule-ride/
- It's a long drive into the North Rim, so plan on spending the night at the lodge or a campground.

The Ten Essentials, Hiking Safety, and Fire

Desert landscapes, like the Grand Canyon, are unforgiving. As always, pack the Ten Essentials: 1) map and compass or GPS device, 2) headlamp or other light, 3) extra clothes, 4) extra water, 5) extra food, 6) matches or a lighter, 7) first-aid kit, 8) knife, 9) shelter, and 10) sun protection.

You can learn more about the Ten Essentials and purchase the items you need at REI.com Whether you are hiking, biking, or just walking around the rim, I advise using hydration packs because they hold more water than a single bottle, and you will tend to drink more water more often.

If you've read book one, you'll have learned that the primary cause of death in the wilderness is falling. And because the Grand Canyon has so many cliffs, side canyons, ridges, and outcrops, it's important to be mindful and aware of your surroundings. I tell my kids, "We don't have to be afraid and overly careful about everything. But let's be alert and wise."

Standing at the edge of the Grand Canyon, you might be tempted to throw or trundle a rock. Don't. There are people on the trails below you, and even a small rock could injure or kill someone. Be weather-aware. Temperatures in the summer can reach over 100 degrees. Summer storms bring with them lightning, and winter brings snow and ice.

Sunscreen is critical because not only are you in the desert, you're at 7,000 feet above sea level.

My dad is great at building fires. In fact, the *To Build a Fire* chapter is based on my experience as a kid and of my dad teaching me to build a fire and respect the power of a fire. Perhaps the most important thing he taught me was to only build them with an adult present.

Would you let your kids hike alone as the kids do in the book?

To be honest, I wouldn't allow them to hike without adult supervision until they were older teenagers. And I wouldn't ever be comfortable with them hiking solo. There's safety in groups, and most backcountry injuries and deaths occur when people are hiking alone. When we hike as a family, we always stay within eyesight of one another. Part of the reason Jake ends up in such bad shape on the South Kaibab Trail is that an adult, like his Aunt Judy, is not there to monitor his condition. I've read some very sad stories about people hiking that same trail and dying of heatstroke. While staying within eyesight is wise, it makes for a dull story. So, I've granted Jake and his friends some special privileges in this series.

Learning to Rock Climb

In the story, both Agate and Amber have learned the technical skills of rock climbing. The best way to learn is to find a local climbing gym or climbing club where you can take lessons.

An Invitation: Reading Like A Kid Again

One of the things I love about writing this story is the

connection to real places and events. That pulls this fictional story out of the fantasy genre and into a more real-world experience. But to really enjoy the story, you're going to have to suspend your disbelief a bit. I invite you to read these like you read Nancy Drew or the Hardy Boys or whatever that book or series was that ignited your imagination and love for reading.

Working Through Difficult Dynamics

Some early readers of the book commented that the kids work through their problems at a high level, perhaps more like twenty-year-olds than thirteen-year-olds. But I believe those kinds of conversations are possible if we practice them with our children. They can gain the skills to engage their emotions and talk them out. In fact, I was inspired to write this paragraph today because I got a text from a neighbor. She explained how our kids (ages 8, 11, and 12) were playing together when they encountered a challenging situation. They sat down and worked things out much like Jake and Amber did in the middle of the book. Our dear neighbor was present with them, but she said the kids led the process, and they did it with insight and compassion.

Hiking to Phantom Ranch and Havasupai Gardens

In April 2020, I hiked down to Phantom Ranch with my good friend Josh. I had never been to the Grand Canyon before, and that experience gave me the vision for this book. Because very few people get to travel below the rim, I wanted to share the beauty and wildness of this place with my readers. If you and your family are planning an adventure down to Phantom Ranch, there are a few important things to know. First, like Jake and his family, you'll want to start early, before sunrise, to avoid the heat of the day. Second, reservations at both the campgrounds and Phantom Ranch are very difficult to get. Phantom Ranch uses a lottery system for reservations, and at the time of this publication (2023), services and lodging are limited due to repairs and renovations. You can find out more at https://www.grandcanyonlodges.com/lodging/phantom-ranch/

To camp at Bright Angel Campground or Havasupai Gardens Campground requires a backcountry permit and reservations through the National Park Service. For more information, visit https://www.nps.gov/grca/planyourvisit/backcountry-permit.htm

However, camping at Mather Campground and the other campgrounds along the rim does not require a backcountry permit and can be reserved at https://www.recreation.gov

Phantom Ranch

Nestled at the bottom of the Grand Canyon, Phantom Ranch is the only lodging facility below the rim. Architect, Mary Colter, designed the cabins of Phantom Ranch to blend into the landscape. To do this, she used natural materials, such as stone from the surrounding areas of Bright Angel Canyon. All the other materials had to be hauled down to the site by mule train. Colter worked for the Fred Harvey Company, a concessionaire that ran lodging and other sites within the national parks, and she retired from her work at the age of seventy-nine. There are seven other structures designed by Ms. Colter at the Grand Canyon.

You're probably wondering about that attic space above the canteen dining hall. I made it up for the story, and there are no windows to a secret room. However, in studying photographs, I noticed that some show a ceiling and others show exposed rafters in the dining room. At some point, the low ceiling must have been torn out to create a more open and expansive feel to the space.

Phantom Ranch is magical. The steep canyon walls, beautiful trees, waters of Bright Angel Creek, the nearby Colorado River, and the old, rustic buildings combine to create one of the most unique places in our national parks.

Stephen Mather

In 1880, when Abe Evans was seventeen, Stephen Mather would have been thirteen years old. By the age of forty-seven (that's how old I am this year), Mather had become a self-made millionaire. Around that time in his life, he visited a few of the national parks and saw that they had been overrun and exploited. He also learned of a group of private businessmen who were working to take over groves of giant sequoias. Mather later went to Washington to see how he could help and was appointed the first director of the National Park Service. He helped expand the parks system, made the parks more accessible to more people, and built a support staff to care for the places he held so dear.

The Black and Silver Bridges

The Kaibab Bridge is better known as the Black Bridge and crosses the Colorado River just east of Phantom Ranch. Before the bridge was built, the only way to cross the river was by taking a cable tram. Imagine being suspended in a metal cage on a cable strung over churning brown waters. President Theodore Roosevelt took the tram ride during his 1913 hunting expedition down in the canyon–and enjoyed the ride. The bridge was built from 1928 to 1929 and spans 550 feet. The tunnel is just over 100 feet long. I had no idea it even existed until I made the hike and was surprised by its dark entrance when I turned the corner of the trail. The tunnel and bridge were extremely demanding to build and an amazing feat of human engineering. You can learn more about the bridge at the National Park Service website: https://www.nps.gov/articles/bridgeworthy.htm

Trans-Canyon Telephone Line

In 1934, the Civilian Conservation Corps (CCC) began building a telephone line to provide communication between the North and South Rims of the Grand Canyon. It ran from the North Rim, down to Phantom Ranch, across the river, and then split into two different lines. One went up to The Tip Off along the South Kaibab Trail and the other to Havasupai Gardens. If you hike the trails into the canyon, you'll encounter some of the abandoned lines and poles used to support them. In the story, Agate connects her ham radio antenna wire to a segment of the line to create a more powerful antenna. I'm not sure if that's really possible, but I thought it was a fun way to incorporate this piece of history into the story.

Ancestral Puebloan Ruins Near Black Bridge

After you step off the Black Bridge and start heading toward Phantom Ranch, you'll encounter an area to the south that was once inhabited by Ancestral Puebloans. This area was built about 1,000 years ago by what was likely an extended family who farmed the area, growing corn and squash. Archeologists theorize that the people left due to changes in climate that caused extended periods of drought, making the area unsustainable for farming. Learn more about this site at the National Parks Service website:

https://www.nps.gov/grca/learn/historyculture/ba-pueblo.htm

Ancestral Puebloans

The Four Corners region of the American Southwest was home to people who built houses, villages, and cliff dwellings from about 2,700 years ago up to about 700 years ago. This group of people has also been called *Anasazi*, which translates in Navajo to "ancient ones" or "ancient enemies." Because of this, present-day Pueblo peoples, who have a deep respect for their ancestors, prefer the more accurate and respectful term, *Ancestral Puebloan*. The best-known and largest sites are found in Mesa Verde National Park in Colorado and Chaco Canyon in New Mexico. However, smaller groups of these people also lived in the Grand Canyon, and archeologists have discovered a variety of artifacts left by them. Some of the oldest are small figurines of deer and bighorn sheep crafted out of willow branches. Some of these may be much older—up to 4,000 years old—and left by hunting and gathering cultures that predate what we know of the Ancestral Puebloans.

There are ruins of ancient wooden bridges in the canyon. The most famous is called the Anasazi Bridge. About 35 miles upstream from Phantom Ranch, you'll find the

Nankoweap Granaries. These were built by Ancestral Puebloans about 900 years ago as a place to store corn and pumpkin seeds, preserving their food from floods and rodents. This inspired the granaries Nahmida and Abe see in the book. You might be wondering about the clay pots they found buried in the ground. I don't know if there is archeological evidence for this; however, there was a raft guide who decided to hike more of the rim than perhaps any other person in modern history. Along his routes, he said that he found ancient paths with old bridges and places where clay pots had been buried in the ground. He concluded that Ancestral Puebloans used these to store food to sustain them during their frequent and long travels.

Around 1300 A.D., the Ancestral Puebloans had largely left their settlements. Archeologists think that this was due to several factors: violence, collapsing trade networks, and drought. However, the evidence is sparse, and the true story remains a mystery. It appears that they moved to the south and east and established new villages. Their descendants are the present-day Pueblo peoples, such as the Acoma, Hopi, and Zuni. Today, about 75,000 Puebloan people live in New Mexico and Arizona, many in Puebloan communities constructed using an architecture similar to the building methods of their ancestors.

The story mentions granaries, structures built with stone and mud along high cliffs where the Ancestral Puebloans would store grains. The drawing of the granary in chapter seventeen is a depiction of the most famous granary in the Grand Canyon called Nankoweap. The granary Amber climbs to just northeast of Havasupai Gardens is not a real location. However, there are granary ruins in the vicinity of Havasupai Gardens.

The Havasupai

The Havasupai people are a Native American tribe who have their own land and still live in the Grand Canyon. Their story is a testimony of perseverance and love for their homeland. I was inspired to share some of their story through the character of Nahmida after reading *I Am the Grand Canyon*, which was written by Stephen Hirst. He and his wife lived with the Havasupai people and joined them in their legal fight to reclaim the ancestral lands on the canyon rim that are so critical to their daily lives.

As a teenager, my family's farm was threatened by a group of men who used underhanded means to take it away from us. My parents had to stand up for themselves and work tirelessly to keep our home. You can imagine that, as a young kid, it was scary. So, when I read stories about the Havasupai and the people who were trying to take away their home, it feels personal, and I want others to know their story, too.

The Havasupai Reservation is located 34 miles northwest (as the crow flies) from Grand Canyon Village. Their village, Supai, is located within the canyon, and there are no roads into the town. For ages, the Havasupai people lived in the canyon during the spring and summer months, when the lower lands could be cultivated. From November through March, when the canyon was too cold and barren, they would live on the plateau and hunt wild game. From about 1880 to 1974, their lands were limited to the confines of the canyon, which was like being caged for the winters and cut off from both their food and way of life. Ranchmen's cattle drank the limited water and overgrazed the plateau lands, driving out the deer and other game the people depended upon to sustain themselves through the long winters. The Havasupai persevered for decades in legal battles to reclaim their land. Finally, in 1975, they won, and their ancestral plateau lands were returned to them.

Havasupai Canyon is both a magical and fragile place. It's famous for its blue and turquoise pools of water and waterfalls that crash over the orange and red cliffs in Havasu Creek. You can visit the canyon and swim in the waters of Havasu Creek by applying for a reservation, and you can even camp down in the canyon. But to get there, you'll have to hike in, ride a mule or horse, or fly in by helicopter.

In the story, we meet three characters with Havasupai names: Nahmida, Hmaañ Gjaah, and Gswedva. Nahmida means "reliable." Hmaañ Gjaah means "Guards the Children," and he was a respected leader of the Havasupai from 1900 until 1942. Gswedva means "Dangling Beard," and he was also a leader and spokesman for the community. He was an imposing figure, standing over six feet tall. Gswedva lived at and farmed what is now Havasupai Gardens until he was forced to leave at eighty years old. In the story, Havasupai Gardens is referred to as *The Place Below the Spruce Trees*, the English translation of its former Havasupai name.

Pictograph at Mallery's Grotto

The pictograph Jake and his friends noticed are located near the first tunnel along the Bright Angel Trail. Several figures of deer are painted in red along an overhang. We believe these were used by people who had lived here to mark a trail down into the canyon. You can see them today by taking a short hike down the trail. Bring some binoculars to get a better view.

Nahmida's Survival Skills

I wish that I could remember where I read about evening thermal winds in the Grand Canyon. I've searched and searched but can't find the source. Here's the idea, though: As the canyon cools, the hot air jets up the sides of certain areas of the canyon, and currents of cool air flow down into it. In the story, Nahmida knows a place where this occurs and uses it to keep them warm through the night. He also finds salt along a canyon wall. While salt deposits are not prevalent in the Grand Canyon, they do exist. The Hopi tribe has a sacred salt mine site about 25 miles upstream from Phantom Ranch. Salt is an electrolyte and would help Abe's dehydrated body absorb the water he needed to recover.

Nahmida also knew where to find beans and squash in abandoned gardens along the North Rim. There is archeological evidence of gardens along the North Rim. As I wrote the story, I imagined that in 1880 these abandoned fields still might have some sparse crops and that Nahmida would know where they were. As a kid, I remember hiking through old homesteads and finding what are called *volunteer* plants coming up out of the ground. I figured that Nahmida did the same thing.

1880 - Abe's Story: A Summary of Books 1 and 2

Spoiler Alert: If you've not read the first two books in the series, this segment might ruin some things for you. Abe is seventeen. He's an orphan who was living in Philadelphia, working in a factory to earn money so that he could buy a train ticket to Colorado. He accomplished that goal and, after arriving in Denver, traveled to Estes Park, where he happened upon some men who were burying an artifact they had stolen from a widow in town. He dug up the item to discover it was an ancient silver spearhead. He took the spearhead and returned it to its rightful owner. However, before he gave it back, he drew a copy of it into his journal. Ever since he had found it, he felt like he was somehow connected to its story.

Abe met an old mountain man, Hank March, and asked him about the spearhead. Hank had heard stories about it and knew that a group of businessmen in Wyoming were searching for it. He also told Abe about something valuable hidden in a cave in the Sangre de Cristo Mountains: a cube made of wood, likely crafted by the Spanish Conquistadors. He shared with Abe that the only way to figure it out was to find a people who lived in the Grand Canyon. So, Abe took the cube and headed to Arizona. But a group of men who were after the spearhead and the cube are pursuing him. That's where our 1880 story in book three picks up.

Download the Vocabulary List

My great-grandfather was a nuclear scientist who worked on the Manhattan Project to build the atomic bomb. He taught me to keep a dictionary nearby when I read a book so that I could look up unfamiliar words and learn their meanings. I also believe that young readers are curious readers, and

I purposefully choose terms that best describe a scene and give readers an opportunity to learn new words. You can download this list of over sixty words and their definitions as a PDF at https://nationalparkmysteryseries.com/vocabularylist03

Download the Extended Chapter

I've written and illustrated an extended version of the *To Build a Fire* chapter. You can download the PDF at https://nationalparkmysteryseries.com/tobuildafire

Acknowledgments

I'd first like to express my gratitude to my wife, Jenah, and daughters, India and Zion, for their support while I worked on this third book. You three are amazing.

The person I credit for keeping me connected to Jake's emotions, and his affection for his grandfather is my editing partner, Susan Rosenbluth. She has also taught me so much about the craft of writing. Avery Simmons Chen has helped me make some of those important cut-or-keep decisions and helped spot continuity issues in my early drafts. Anna Staver provided the first developmental edit. I'm grateful to have such an amazing team of editors.

I'm deeply indebted to all of my beta readers. This was a more challenging story to right, and your feedback was invaluable: Susan Simomns, Crystal Green, Preston Lastowski, Caroline Hermann, Amanda Cross, Elaine Sestito, Delene Gillespie, Amanda Wandres, Olivia Simmons, Paxton Fussman, Christine Mandiloff, Catherine Haws, Rianna Vandergaast Zeilstra, Patrick Zeilstra, Luca Sherman, Kim Self, Elijah Oudin, Rebecca Kleveland, Aarav Mugur, Diana Wilson, Patrick Massey, Anell Massey, Terri Avenarius, Nancy Lee Zimpleman, Lara LaChapelle, and Denise Herbert.

For this book, I crowdsourced my proofreading. And there were at least three hundred errors the team identified and corrected. I'd like to express a special thanks to Carri Boerema, who spotted and corrected about 80% of the errors. Thank you for your encouragement and help: Jennifer Sebranek, Nancy Lee, Elissa Choma, Caroline Hermann, Rachel Bertagnoli, Susan Johnson, Lindsy McKnight, Tracy Pickering, Nicole Pringle, Amanda Wandres, Christine Mandiloff, Ashlee Folsom, Lana Hamby, and Abigail Fefferman.

I want to thank my launch team of educators, librarians, and national park lovers. If you'd like to join one of the launch teams for future books, you can sign up at: https://nationalparkmysteryseries.com/launchteam

I'm deeply indebted to author Stephen Hirst and the Havauspai people who have shared their lives with me in the book, *I Am The Grand Canyon.* It is a labor of love and a masterpiece.

Finally, I'd like to thank the rangers who serve at Grand Canyon National Park.

If You Enjoyed The Story...

If you enjoyed this story, I would appreciate your help getting copies into the hands of families and other young people. Here are a few ways you can do that:

- **Write a review** on Amazon and Goodreads.
- **Review Writing Tips:** A) Share your experience. What was it like for you to read and experience the story? B) It's a mystery, so try not to post any spoilers. C) If you read the book with a young person, describe what they enjoyed most about the story.
- **Upvote your favorite reviews.** On Amazon, you can *like* the reviews that you find most helpful. This helps to feature those reviews that best serve potential readers.
- **Loan** or give your copy to a friend.

- **Ask your local library** to acquire the series in their collection.
- **Purchase a copy.** They make great gifts. I'll be narrating the audiobooks, so look for those on my author page on audible: https://www.audible.com/author/Aaron-Johnson/B086W2DTMT
- **Post on social media.** You can get links and images to post at https://nationalparkmysteryseries.com/launchteam
- **Share your copy with others.**
- **Connections**: I'd greatly appreciate it if you would connect me with people you know who may be able to help me promote the book and the series. You can make an introduction by emailing me at **aaron@nationalparkmysteryseries.com**
- By the way, if you promote the books in some way, **email me** to let me know. As a way to say thank you, I've got a small gift to send your way.
- **Bulk Orders:** If you would like to place a bulk order at reduced pricing, reach out to me via email. Bulk orders start at ten books or more.
- **Speaking**: I would enjoy the opportunity to speak via Zoom or in-person with large and small groups. Wilson Rawls, author of *Where the Red Fern Grows*, spoke at thousands of schools. I hope to do the same.

- Visit https://nationalparkmysteryseries.com to discover more ways to engage with the series.

Also by the Author

Book 1: *Mystery in Rocky Mountain National Park*

Book 2: *Discovery in Great Sand Dunes National Park*

Book 3: *Adventure in Grand Canyon National Park*

Book 4: *Zion National Park* - Scheduled for 2023 Publication.

Book 5: *Yosemite National Park* - Scheduled for 2023 Publication.

Book 6: *Mt. Rainier National Park* - Scheduled for 2023 Publication.

Book 7: *Olympic National Park* - Scheduled for 2023 Publication.

Book 8: *Glacier National Park* - Scheduled for 2024 Publication.

Book 9: *Yellowstone National Park* - Scheduled for 2024 Publication.

Book 10: *Grand Teton National Park* - Scheduled for 2024 Publication.

Into the Rainforest: Book 1 in the Lost City Series

https://NationalParkMysterySeries.com

While You're Waiting...

I'd like to recommend a wonderful book written by my daughter, India Johnson. You can purchase a copy at Amazon at https://amzn.to/3KSj26D or search for Rebels' Daughter.

When twelve-year-old Sky sneaks out one night, her whole world changes. On accident, she makes an enemy that will stop at nothing to destroy her family and humankind. Her parents are leaders of the rebellion, fighting against those who plan to enslave the last humans. That means that she has to be extra careful. Something she's not. Sky runs from talking wolves and crickcrawks, asking many questions about what's happening to her. Why are her things disappearing? Will she ever convince everyone that she can lead? And when something unexpected happens, she must face the most important question of all. Will she ever get home? Written by twelve-year-old (now fourteen) author, India Johnson, this is her first novel in the *Freedom Through Fire Saga*.

Proud Parent Note: India was the recipient of a Scholastic Art and Writing Regional Gold Key award for *The Rebels' Daughter.*

About the Author

As I've hiked throughout different national parks and my home of Colorado, I've imagined stories about young boys and girls searching for treasure and, in the process, discovering the best treasure of all: the beauty of wild places. I've been inspired by my own searches for a treasure in the gorges and caves of Ohio, and by my dad, who discovered an ancient Native American settlement when he was just a teenager.

I've always loved stories, but I didn't always love reading. That changed in sixth grade when my teacher, Mrs. Jones, gave me a copy of *The Book of Three* by Lloyd Alexander. I hope that the books in my series awaken a love for reading in kids just as that book did for me.

I believe that the best way to care for our natural treasures is to first develop a deep connection with them. I hope you have been able to do so in these pages, and that you'll be able to get outside to develop an even deeper affection for the outdoors and national parks near you.

You can contact me at aaron@nationalparkmysteryseries.com

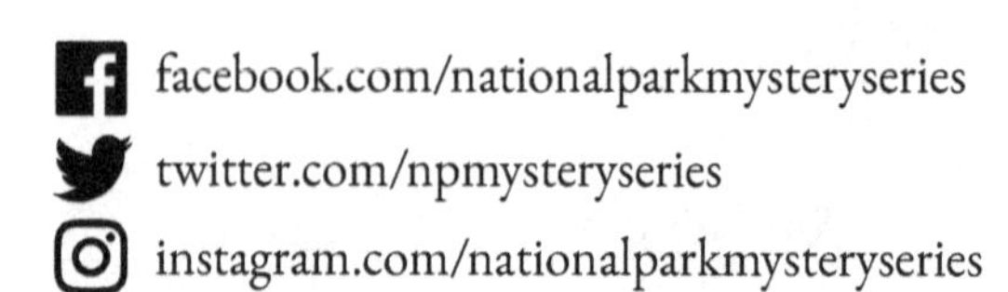
facebook.com/nationalparkmysteryseries
twitter.com/npmysteryseries
instagram.com/nationalparkmysteryseries

Printed in the USA
CPSIA information can be obtained
at www.ICGtesting.com
BVHW041909200823
668717BV00005B/43